SOUTH CALIFORNIA PURPLES

SOUTH CALIFORNIA PURPLES

BARON R. BIRTCHER

THE PERMANENT PRESS
Sag Harbor, NY 11963

For information, address:
The Permanent Press
4170 Noyac Road
Sag Harbor, NY 11963
www.thepermanentpress.com

Library of Congress Cataloging-in-Publication Data

Birtcher, Baron R., author.
    South California purples / Baron R. Birtcher.
    Sag Harbor, NY : The Permanent Press, [2017]
    ISBN 978-1-57962-500-9 (hardcover)
        1. City and town life—Oregon—Fiction. 2. Ranchers—
Oregon—Fiction. 3. Nineteen seventies—Fiction.

PS3552.I7573 S67 2017
813'.54—dc23   2016053021

Printed in the United States of America

This one's for my Dad

"I thought I met a man
Who said he knew a man
Who knew what was going on
I was mistaken . . ."

—DAVID CROSBY, "Laughing"

———~~~———

"You will know them by their fruits . . ."

—MATTHEW 7:16
New American Standard Bible

NEW YEAR'S
1973

IT IS SAID that history is defined by the things we never saw coming. I have found that to be true.

There was a peculiar feeling in the air that year, and it seemed to be seeping into every corner of our lives. Newspapers reported events using language that reeked of malaise, sapped of any revenant of the joy that had once accompanied the birth pangs of the Age of Aquarius.

The last of America's soldiers were finally on their way home—Vietnamization—though they were coming home alone rather than together with their units, victorious brigades returning to home shores, as had been done at the conclusion of prior wars. These soldiers had been spat upon by protestors who gathered at airports and shouted insults and epithets and labeled the young, dazed soldiers as "baby killers" all while the stench of smoke and white phosphorous still permeated the fabric of the uniforms they wore; some not even forty-eight hours from the scene of their final firefight, nor more than twenty years of age. But lately it was as though even the hippies and freaks had lost their fervor for the end of this conflict, and no longer wished to celebrate the accomplishment by spitting on their victims.

To me, it marked the incipient mortality of the values that I had taken for granted as a younger man, when I had returned from my generation's war. I feared what would come to fill the vacuum left behind.

I felt too young to be harboring judgments such as these; they belonged inside the minds of much older men, to the graybeards who gathered themselves in lodges that bore the names of animals, and who played checkers while complaining of physical maladies and retold stories of misremembered histories and tales of conquests that never happened at all. Like those men, I will always carry my war with me, but the marks that had been blazed upon the trunks of old-growth forests, the ones that branded the narrow line between passion and disaster, were beginning to fade away.

The shape and nature of war had changed.

As had the nature of peace.

———

MY WIFE and I watched the ball drop in New York City where the murder rate had just reached an all-time high, heroin was the drug of choice, and teenaged prostitutes worked openly on every corner of Times Square. We watched it from the safe distance afforded by the television console in the living room at the ranch, while the fire in the hearth cracked and funneled fragrant plumes of smoke out into the snow-blanketed Oregon night. I popped a bottle of iced champagne and kissed her as the band played "Auld Lang Syne" and '72 went into the books.

The old year was gone.

Nixon had gone to China, and Jane Fonda straddled a North Vietnamese antiaircraft gun for the enjoyment of the press corps; in June, five Nixon campaign operatives had been arrested after breaking into the Watergate Complex, and by

August, the last United States ground troops were promised to begin returning home from 'Nam; Bobby Fischer defeated Boris Spassky in a chess match viewed by millions all over the world, and American eighteen-year-olds won the right to vote and celebrated that newfound gift by delivering Richard Nixon a landslide second-term presidency that recorded the lowest voter turnout in nearly three decades.

Baby New Year had arrived, but we had no way of knowing at the moment that the restless little bastard had been delivered into this world with the myopic inclinations of a narcissist, and in possession of the heart of a cynic.

——⟊⟊⟊——

I CANNOT lay claim, with any specificity, to know what evil is. I had seen it in Korea and encountered its image and affect in the random acts of scared and desperate men. Sometimes they invaded my sleep and revealed themselves inside the rippling waves that rose from the flames of a human form torched in effigy. Other times, even on a bright spring day, with the sun burning warm and yellow behind a patch of cumulus as it floated above the valley, I could feel its foul breath against the skin on the back of my neck. These were the intrusions I had come to fear the most.

PART ONE:
SPRING WORKS

CHAPTER ONE

A NARROW STRIP of orange appeared along the ridgeline as the glow of the rising sun refracted off the clouds that lay inside the folds of the Cascades. I pulled at the wool collar of my jacket and turned my horse away from the brittle oncoming wind that still carried the reminder of winter.

We had been riding since well before sunrise in the hopes that we'd make the upper pasture before the first full flush of dawn stirred the cattle and made the job of gathering the herd all the more difficult. I looked off behind me and watched my best roper, Jordan Powell, work his way through a heavy growth of brush toward the cluster of cows that had taken shelter with their calves in the lee of a rock cove. His roan gelding was blowing puffs of white fog from its nostrils and the vapor of Powell's own breath hovered around his head and reflected the pale sunlight.

The winter had been a long one, and we were getting a late start on spring. It was already the first week of April, and we should have cleared at least half of my outlying pastures of grazing stock by now, and brought them back to the pens for health checks, sorting, and counting.

I whistled softly to my dog, Wyatt, a blue heeler who lived for the chance to work the herd. He came to attention and waited for my command, his eyes locked on me.

"Away to me," I said, and he immediately sprang to his feet and started a wide circle around the small group of heifers I was working.

I untied my loop from the saddle and moved in a flanking arc that would cut off their only route of escape. I momentarily lost sight of both Powell and his separate portion of the herd as I passed behind the rise of the rock outcropping, but I heard him clearly enough.

"Sonofabitch," he said.

I spurred my horse into the gap and got my first look at the mutilated, nearly unrecognizable corpse of one of my cattle.

"Goddammit, Captain," Powell said.

"Cussing my dead cow isn't gonna bring her back."

"I'm not cussing your dead cow. I'm cussing whatever killed her. That's what, four in the last two weeks?"

"And three others over near the Corcoran piece."

I strung the reata over my saddle horn and dismounted, handing the reins to Powell as I moved closer to the corpse, or what was left of it. Our horses were balky with the smell of blood and Powell eased them back as I circled around on foot to get a better look. A couple of guys with a Winchester rifle, a pickup, and a chainsaw can butcher a cow and disappear in minutes. But like the others, this didn't have that appearance, plus it was miles over muddy, rough, and rocky terrain in order to get to my access road, let alone back to the highway.

"They didn't take away any meat," I said.

"Don't know how they coulda got any. Looks to me like the damn thing blew apart."

"The head's gone," I said. "I don't see it anywhere. You?"

Powell made a slow pass in the dew-covered grass, my horse still trailing behind him, and we separately searched all the way to the fence line. Wyatt remained focused on his job, paying no attention to either Powell or me, loose-herding his group and moving them in the direction of the ranch.

"I don't see it, either," he said. "Can't imagine anybody came out all this way for a skull and a set of horns."

"Well," I said. "I tell you what: it's not coyotes. No animal could have done this kind of damage."

I dipped into my pocket and came out with a cigarette, turned my back to the wind, and lit it, watched the gray smoke tear away in the breeze. I pocketed my Zippo and took a folding shovel from my saddlebag.

The morning sun illuminated the planes and creases of Powell's face as he eyed the trenching tool.

"What are you gonna do with that?"

"You come on down here with me, and I'll show you," I said.

"You hired me for a cowhand, Captain. I reckon if I can't do it ahorseback, it can't need doing all that bad."

"If you don't get down off that animal and help me dig a hole for this cow, I guarantee that you'll have plenty of time to do your reckoning while you walk your ass back to the ranch," I said.

"Somebody's got to keep hold of these horses."

"I suspect you could tie them to one of those trees down there, and they'll be patient enough for a while."

Powell chewed his bottom lip as he looked down the slope toward the poplars that grew along the river, and shook his head. After a moment, he clucked his roan and headed off toward a stand of sugar pines. I finished my smoke, field-stripped it, and tucked the dead filter back into the pocket of my jeans.

"Better jangle those spurs, Jordan," I said. "This hole isn't going to dig itself."

—————

THE SUN was well up and had burned the chill from the air by the time we gathered the herd and hazed them through the trees, and up over the crest of the rise that looked down on the main body of my ranch. I had been raised on this land, watched the whole county grow up from between the ears of a horse.

Family legend had it that my grandfather acquired his first quarter section in exchange for fifty dollars and a shotgun from an Ohio man who decided he didn't want the piece he'd claimed. That was 1895. Granddad constructed a small house and spent every dollar he made adding to his holdings in both land and livestock, earning a reputation as tough but hard-hewn, and a fixture of stability in Meriwether County. He was there selling rough stock the day that Bonnie McCarroll was beaten to death by a bronc at the Pendleton roundup in 1929, the same day my father got married to my mother. I was born three years later.

I worked the ranch every day until I went to college on an ROTC scholarship and did my bit in Korea as the captain of an MP unit, which consisted of every manner of drunk, troublemaker, and knucklehead who had managed to get himself washed out of his original platoon and have his sorry ass sent over to me. Not a day went by that I did not think about returning to this place.

By the time I did make it back, my father was dead from an aneurism, but not before he had aggregated over 63,000 deeded acres, plus another 14,000 he leased from the Bureau of Land Management. I moved into the main house and took over the operation of the ranch, and kept an eye on my grieving mom for what turned out to be the final two years of her life.

"It's so quiet up here, I swear I can hear the ground squirrels blink their eyes," Powell said, startling me out of my thoughts.

I nodded and lit another cigarette as his horse shook its head and rattled his curb chain.

"Enjoy it while you can," I said. "I believe Dub Naylor's coming back for the Spring Works."

"Aw, damn, Captain."

"Well, ain't you a daisy," I said.

"I swear that old fool could talk the bark off a tree."

"Then I suggest you move your war bag and bedroll to the far side of the bunkhouse. It's fixing to get a little noisier in there."

"Caleb's been hiring?"

"All day long," I said. "Ought to have a decent crew filled out by tomorrow."

"Well, hell."

"Take a look around you, Jordan. It's springtime, son. What do you think we've been doing out here anyway?"

The calves were rooting aimlessly in the clump grass while I took a last look out toward the grove of white oaks that marked the family plot where my entire bloodline lay buried. I whistled to the dog, then reined my horse, and swung a wide circle around the herd and started them moving down the hill.

———

CALEB WHEELER was seated at a spool table in the shade of an atlas cedar, his sweat-stained Stetson pulled low on his brow and obscuring his face in shadow.

"You get yourself some experience and proper headgear, you can come try me again next year," I heard Wheeler say to one of the applicants.

I nodded to the young cowboy as he passed me by, dejected. He couldn't have been old enough to own a razor. I watched him climb into the cab of a faded green pickup and toss his cap on the seat and pull out of the driveway inside a cloud of dust.

My foreman licked the tip of his pencil and scrawled something on a yellow legal pad as I approached the table.

"You want to tell me why this gets harder every year?" Caleb said to me. He leaned back in his folding chair, crossed his arms, and squinted at me through the dappled sunlight. "Pull up a pew, you'll see what I mean."

"What was wrong with that kid?"

"He was wearing a ball cap, for Chrissakes. Are we branding beeves or playing baseball out here?" he said. He looked past me and waved the next applicant over. "Besides, the kid still had California all over his boots."

I took a chair at the spool table and watched a tall, loose-limbed man swing down from his perch on the porch rail of the office and crunch across the gravel toward us. He removed his hat and placed it on the table, crown down. His grip was firm and dry when he offered me his hand.

"Samuel Thomas Griffin," he said. "You must be Mr. Dawson."

"That's right. Tyler Dawson," I offered. "And this over here is Caleb Wheeler, my foreman. Have a seat."

Wheeler pushed the brim of his hat off his brow with a knuckle and eyed the new man. "You get more than your share of lip from the boys, I expect."

"Because I'm black?"

"It is one of your more distinguishing qualities," Wheeler said. "Answer the question."

"Once per man, typically," Griffin smiled. "That usually puts the finish to it."

"He's not kidding, amigo. We don't have time for nonsense," I said. "We got eight weeks to get this herd sorted, horned, and branded."

"It don't ever start with me."

"Good," Wheeler said, loud enough for everybody to hear. "Because if we have one lick of trouble from any of you cowprods, I will run you off this place so fast it'll take your shadow a week to catch up to you."

A cloud of dust from the paddock curled across the open space on a breeze that carried the odor of singed hide and the bawl of a startled calf.

"How much of this kind of work you done before, Griffin?" I asked him.

"I've done a bit. I can set a horse and throw a loop."

I saw the skin at the corner of Wheeler's eyes go tight as he searched the black man's face. "My daughter can do that."

"Then you ought to hire her."

Wheeler tapped his pencil on the legal pad and looked up at a pair of scrub jays scrapping inside the branches of the cedar.

"What do you know about cattle?" I asked.

"Well, sir, it's been awhile, but if I recall correctly, the grass goes in the eyeball end and comes out the other."

Wheeler dropped the pencil and leaned in on his elbows, toward Griffin. "Are you sassing us?"

Griffin smiled, and he looked from me to Wheeler.

"No, sir, just having a little fun. Truth is, I s'pose I can toss a loop as well as any man you got here. First-string linebacker at Cal State Chico don't exactly put you in contention for the NFL. But I did learn my share about animal husbandry."

My foreman stood, placed two fingers in his mouth, and issued a shrill whistle. "Taj! Powell! Get your asses over here!"

Two of my permanent cowboys ran over from the separating pen and skidded to a stop at the edge of the table.

"Get this man a skin string so he can show us what he's got."

We both climbed up and took a seat on the paddock fence, and watched. Within ten minutes, Griffin had roped, dragged, and branded three of the new North Camp calves all by himself. His movements were as confident and fluid as I had ever seen.

Wheeler smoothed his mustache with a thumb and forefinger and pursed his lips as Griffin dusted off his chaps and ambled back toward us.

"You've worked Purples before?" Wheeler asked him.

"Yes, sir," Griffin grinned. "Down in Cali, outside of Paso Robles."

"That's the line these come from," I said. "Long time ago."

"Is the interview over then?"

Wheeler nodded.

"My man Powell over there'll take you to pick out a couple horses from the remuda," he said.

"When you're done with that, go get your gear and find yourself a bunk, Griffin," I added and shook his hand again. "Glad to have you with us."

CHAPTER TWO

JUST PAST NOON, on a ranch many miles south of us, the first of the government trucks appeared.

Teresa Pineu narrowed her eyes and saw the trail of powder their tires kicked up off the hard-packed caliche road that cut along the wire fence that marked the border between her parcel and the BLM. She dried her hands on a dish towel and reached for the binoculars that rested on the ledge beside the trailer's kitchen sink.

The trucks bore no markings, but made no effort toward concealment, though their distinctive shape made clear the nature of the cargo they carried.

So this is how it begins, she thinks.

―◈◈◈―

WILD HORSES had roamed the landscape since the Pleistocene era, but the bloodline that marked this herd could be traced back to the arrival of the first Conquistadores in the fifteenth century. The ocean voyage from Spain was long and arduous, and many of the animals lost their lives, so it was natural that only the strongest, most robust would survive, serve, flourish, and procreate on the shores of the New World.

Somewhat smaller than many of their European counter-parts, but larger than the animals favored by the indigenous population, they thrived in the new environment and were prized for their speed, agility, stamina, and conformation.

Battles were fought, wars won and lost, ranches overrun, and rough stock stolen; but the truth was in their blood. They served and died by the tens of thousands in the armies of the Civil War, the Spanish-American and Boer Wars; more than 500,000 of these fine animals perished in World War I alone, thousands more exterminated just for their hides during the years of the Great Depression.

Still many survived and escaped into the meadows and river valleys, gathering into herds of their own construction. Of these, some made it farther west, through treacherous Rocky Mountain passes drifted deep with ice and snow, and on to survive the waterless desert wastes of Utah, Nevada, and Arizona, eventually to find safe pasture in the verdant wilds of Oregon.

——◦✕◦——

THE NATION was expanding, as well.

Vast tracts of land were purchased, stolen outright, or con-fiscated and partitioned as a spoil of war.

Some was given away as an incentive offered to adventurers and settlers. Considerably more was set aside as a public trust to be overseen by governmental agencies mandated to preserve, protect, and manage its possessions. Perhaps predictably, it was this third objective which was to precipitate an ongoing strug-gle between the rights of private citizens and the bureaucracies engaged to oversee the protection of its resources that would engender ironic, frequent, armed, and bloody conflict.

——◦✕◦——

TERESA PINEU put down the binoculars and stepped outside. The air was cool and dry, the dome of sky strewn with a chain of white clouds. She followed the passage of the distant vehicles until all trace had disappeared, the trail of dust torn away on the wind.

She had heard the rumors for some time, but had chosen to believe they were nothing more, and that a more enlightened perspective had gained a foothold in the world. She now believed she had been a fool to have engaged in such a fantasy.

The last time something like this had transpired was just after the turn of the century. Teresa had seen the faded tintypes of the carnage, and had wondered as to why the perpetrators would have failed to do their evil outside the presence of photographers. But this was the vanity of man. The government had determined that the wild mustang population had exceeded optimal allowances, and therefore threatened the viability of the herd's own survival.

Teresa knew the slaughter would occur much as it had before. This, too, was the vanity of man.

The trucks would be first to arrive, hauling a payload of steel poles and wire that would be formed into makeshift corrals. The private contractors—mercenary drovers and stockmen hired by the government and funded by tax dollars—would follow: accepting their pieces of silver in exchange for scouring the rock-strewn country on horseback, motorcycles, and aircraft for evidence of the herd, then methodically forcing it westward where the animals would find themselves imprisoned inside massive manmade enclosures, denied freedom for the first time in their lives. Some of these men would be issued permits for the privilege of "hunting" the horses with firearms.

When they were finished, the unwanted animals would be eradicated, swallowed up inside refrigerated trucks and processed for use in canned food for our pets, and rawhide chew toys for their amusement.

Teresa turned her head skyward, breathed deeply, and contemplated the flight of a red-tailed hawk as it traced circles on the slipstream. Then she stepped inside and placed a call.

CHAPTER THREE

M Y WIFE, Jesse, was spreading compost and red bark dust in the vegetable garden when I came back to the house. She wore a wide-brimmed straw hat, blue jeans, and a sleeveless blouse, her left cheek marked with a dark smudge where she had wiped away the sheen of perspiration with a soiled glove.

"How goes the search for the world's finest cowboy?" she smiled.

"You're looking at him."

She leaned the rake handle against a tomato stake and stood on her toes to kiss me. The late afternoon sun shone on her bare arms and highlighted the dusting of freckles on her skin, and her hair smelled of green apples and musk.

I kicked at a channel of loose soil with the toe of my boot where a family of voles had bored furrows between the seed rows.

"We lost another cow," I said.

"I know."

"Did Powell come over to tattle?"

Lately, tiny lines had begun to appear at the corners of her eyes and mouth when she smiled. I had met Jesse shortly after I returned home from Korea. I had taken a job as a wrangler on a movie set where she was working as a location scout. It took me a week to work up the courage to ask her if she'd join me for dinner. By the time we'd finished dessert that night, I could not envision a future that didn't have her in it.

"No," she said. "I was over by the sorting pen when you brought in the calves. I could see that one of them was an orphan."

I looked down the slope, in the direction of the pens where the hands were finishing their work with the day's final group of calves. Wyatt was trotting up the dirt track, his tongue hanging loosely from his mouth, and an expression on his face that I'd swear resembled a smile. He wagged his tail and circled Jesse and me, and I bent down to scratch him behind his ears before he walked off in search of shade beneath the porch.

"I love that sound, don't you?" Jesse asked.

We both listened as the voice of the iron tender shouted out the last of the calves, and the hollers of the crew of cutters, branders, and vaccinators worked together in the chaotic and rough-hewn opera that defined the season. A minute later, a diaphanous bulb of gray smoke carried through the tree limbs when they killed the branding fire with metal pails of well water, and the smell of singed hair and superheated steam followed behind.

"You are a country girl," I said. "You probably like the stink of a farrier's shed."

"You know I do." She smiled and wrapped an arm around my waist.

Jordan Powell waved his arm and shouted something I couldn't quite hear from where he stood between the trees and the horse barn. He was carrying something up the gravel path toward Jesse and me, wearing leather work chaps and a snap-button shirt that were powdered with dust. The Resistol hat he wore was banded with a stain of sweat along the crown.

"Miz Dawson," he said and touched his fingers to the brim.

"Long day, Jordan?" she asked.

"Yes, ma'am. But I didn't break no bones, so I guess it was a good one."

"Don't be too long," Jesse said to me as she turned to go inside. "We're going to the Corcorans' tonight, and you're not going anywhere with me if you don't take a shower. And soon."

It had become our custom to go visit with our nearest neighbors at least once a month and bring a casserole, a side of ribs, or some other form of home-cooked sustenance and a little conversation to the father-and-son set of bachelors who now lived alone: one a widower, the other a cuckold. It was a kindness I credited exclusively to Jesse's compassionate nature.

The kitchen door squeaked on its hinges as Jesse pulled on the handle, and Wyatt jumped up to follow her inside.

"You left your duster down by the barn," Powell told me once Jesse had disappeared indoors. "Figured you'd want it."

"I appreciate it."

"One other thing: Mr. Wheeler's sending me and the new man, Griffin, out to the Three Roses parcel tomorrow to root out the cows hiding in the trees up there. He asked me to see if you thought you'd want to come along."

I appreciated what Wheeler was trying to do. Running a family operation is a complicated business, and while Caleb Wheeler had been my foreman for more than a decade, there was still a balance to be observed between who was the boss and who was in charge. A ranch is a business, but it's also a family.

Powell looked off in the direction of the ranch office and chewed a hangnail off his thumb.

"No," I said. "You boys can handle it on your own. It'll be good for you to get to know Griffin anyway. He looks like he's got the makings of a permanent hand."

"Whatever you say, Captain."

Powell looked like he was about to speak again, but checked himself.

"Something else on your mind?" I asked.

"No, sir," he said and turned back toward the barn. The rowels of his spurs rang like tiny bells as he slowly walked away.

FOR MY fortieth birthday, a year ago, my wife surprised me with the gift of a brand-new 1972 Ford Bronco. Its body was the color of the river when it ran deep and blue, and had white fenders and a top I removed when the weather was good. She'd had a local sign painter ornament each of the two doors with a representation of our ranch's brand, a capital D enclosed within the outline of a diamond. The Diamond-D. We referred to it as our Sunday car, in that Jesse had developed an unwillingness to be seen in my work truck, or the military surplus jeep I sometimes used to haul tools around the property, when we drove to church on Sundays. It had since expanded its role to include transport to any social occasion that involved nonranch personnel.

I held the door open for Jesse as she settled herself into the passenger seat, balancing the casserole dish and pie plate on her lap while I placed the bundle of handpicked flowers on the seat.

Back in the early twenties, when the country was booming with postwar expansion, my grandfather had taken an uncharacteristic long-shot risk on a new breed of cattle that had shown early promise in its resistance to certain bovine diseases and produced a richly marbled, tender beef product that was beginning to bring top dollar at auction. Neighboring ranchers considered him crazy to bet on livestock that had not been tested in climates less temperate than Southern California, and felt free to let him know about it. But the gamble paid off and, largely due to their robust health, the herd grew far more rapidly than those on any other ranch in the state. The Diamond-D came to be widely known for the quality of the beef that derived from this unusual crossbreed of Welsh Black and Tarentaise cows that carried a hide so dark that they appeared nearly purple in direct sunlight.

As a cattleman, his neighbor Eli Corcoran had not been so fortunate.

He and my granddad had planted their stakes about the same time, starting out with a few hundred acres, and sharing a boundary that defined the northern border of Corcoran's place and the southern border of the Diamond-D. They were affable competitors who developed a mutual respect for one another as the years progressed. Both men married good women, raised sons, and worked their respective properties with the tirelessness of much younger men. But the Great War came and claimed the oldest Corcoran boy. Eli missed the boom when it came to an end, and found himself unprepared when the depression came.

Granddad proved his friendship by purchasing small parcels—parcels my grandfather had no need for—of Corcoran's ranch to provide his friend the cash he needed to keep going. Eli worked his shrinking property with the help of his only remaining son, Denman, who had earned the nickname "Snoose" since that was what they would most frequently find him doing if they left him alone to work a string, or mend a length of fence. By the time the Second War came along, Corcoran was down to his last one hundred acres, which he offered for sale to my family.

Grandfather refused, and offered instead to lease the acreage for grazing. The payment on that lease continues to this day, the only thing that stands between the Corcorans and outright destitution.

———

THE FIRST stars had only begun to reveal themselves in the early evening sky, the moon a thin white crescent rising over the horizon, and my headlights exaggerated the shadows of the washboard ruts etched in the surface of the road.

Like most locales in this valley, the simplest way to get to the Corcoran place was on horseback. A horse trail ran the length of the wire fence that enclosed the BLM land to the east of us and straight to the Corcorans' back gate. But the trail was far too narrow, and far too rough, to accommodate a motor vehicle, especially this time of year. Instead we took the longer route over a road meant for use by delivery trucks that had been carved out of hardpan and gravel, and was now deeply scalloped by years of rainfall and neglect.

I cast a glance at Jesse as we rumbled over the cattle guard and underneath the lodgepole arch that identified the entrance to the Corcoran ranch. As I turned toward the house, my lights brushed across the desiccated skin of a coyote, which had been strung up on the barbed-wire fence as a warning to the rest of the pack.

A Massey Ferguson tractor was parked inside a lean-to shed with no doors, whose wooden exterior had gone gray with weather and dripping moisture from holes in the roof where the wind had stripped it of shingles. Farm implements lay exposed in the open, bled rust, and gave the appearance of dead or dying insects from a distant geological age.

I parked beneath a walnut tree that grew on the near side of the house. A thick layer of green moss encrusted its trunk and exposed roots like a second skin.

Several years ago, before Eli's wife, Marie, had passed away, he had taken down the wood-framed house he had first built as a young man, and replaced it with one constructed out of river rock, heavy timber, and mortar. It was built up off the ground on broad redwood posts and beams that had been sunk deep into concrete footings, much like the pilings of a pier. The sagging treads of the original stairway, and the wood stoop they led up to, though, were a monument to the interest he lost in completing the project after she had died.

This was where Eli and his sixty-one-year-old son, Snoose Corcoran, were seated as Jesse and I got out of the Bronco.

Despite the property's decrepitude, the evening air was sweet, laced with the smell of rain-dampened soil, bailed hay, and the spilled contents of feed sacks.

Eli Corcoran removed his straw Stetson as Jesse came up the stairs.

"Miss Jesse," he said, and smiled, and some of the weariness slid off of him.

"You know you make me feel like a matron when you call me that," Jesse said.

She leaned in and pecked him on the cheek and I could see a flicker of youth hidden deep in his eyes when he put his hat back on.

"Can't help it," the old man said. "I was raised by proper Baptist parents who taught me to show respect for a lady."

I shook hands with Snoose and noticed again the resemblance between father and son. Both had the angular faces and suntanned complexions of their Black Irish ancestors, and shared the deep lines that had been chiseled on their cheekbones; but the old man's eyes were red along the rims and the bone structure of his face had hollowed out. He had shaved in preparation for our visit, and his chin had been nicked by the razor, a scrap of toilet paper still stuck to the wound.

Snoose, too, looked tired, his eyes shot through with the swollen look of worry and deprivation from sleep. Unlike Eli, it looked as though Snoose hadn't shaved for days, and the smell of Kentucky brown seemed to emanate from his pores.

"Why don't you take those flowers inside," Eli said to Jesse. "Miss Marie can give you a hand finding something to put them in."

A momentary expression of confusion passed over Jesse's features, before a simple sadness took its place.

Snoose shot me a look that contained an entire conversation.

"Let me give you a hand with that food," Snoose said. He took the casserole and pie from me and followed Jesse inside.

"Pull up a seat, Dawson," Eli said, and gestured to the willow chair his son had been using.

He pulled a plug of tobacco from his shirt pocket, flaked some off with the edge of a pocket knife, and rolled himself a smoke while I listened to the low murmur of conversation mingle with the rattle of cookware that drifted through an aluminum screen door decorated with scrollwork and the images of swallows in flight.

"You going to speak to the sheriff about those dead cows?" Eli asked.

He lit a wooden match with a flick of his thumbnail and touched it to the end of his cigarette. He inhaled deeply as he waved the match dead and dropped it to the floor.

"Yes, sir," I said. "Planning on calling him tomorrow."

"Don't you let him slow-walk this thing. It's damn serious. I ain't seen nothing like it before."

"I haven't either."

He stopped for a moment and gazed out into the dusk, blinking like he was seeing something there, the images of lost friends squinting into the gleam of a meat fire spinning stories and lies from the trail. He picked a piece of loose tobacco off his tongue and wiped his fingertips on the leg of his blue jeans.

"These animals suffer—or not—depending on our choices, son. We can choose whether their last day is a good one or a bad one."

"I share your feeling on that, sir," I said.

"It ain't a feeling, it's a *code*, goddamn it."

He came back to himself then, took a last draw from his hand-roll and crushed it beneath the sole of his boot.

"I tell you what," he said. The lines at the edges of his eyes grew deeper as he gazed at me. "In my day, we didn't waste a lot of time between the rustling and the hanging."

"I don't plan on lingering."

"I know you don't. It's Lloyd Skadden I'm worrying on. You know, Dawson, I knew that boy's granddaddy. He was a good man, like yours was. Your daddy, too. But Lloyd? I never knew what was in that boy's head."

"I can't say I know him very well, myself."

"Me, neither, but what I do know is that he ain't hobbled by being too modest, or by too much hard work, either."

———◈◈◈———

"WE CAN eat here on the porch," Snoose said as he brought the stove-warmed food out from the kitchen. "It's a pleasant evening out."

A plank picnic table covered in red-and-white checked oil-cloth had been set in the far corner where the living room window spilled light out into the night.

I took a hold of Eli's elbow, and he let me help him up out of his chair. The old man may have shaved, but he hadn't bathed that day, and a smell like spoiled milk floated up out of the wrinkles in his shirt.

Jesse served supper onto a set of chipped and mismatched plates with a metal serving spoon. A pitcher of iced lemonade stood at the center of the table, dripping condensation in a pool that ran off the edge and onto the uneven boards of the floor.

Eli said grace for all of us, and we talked and ate and listened to his stories of drovers and transient cowhands on the Goodnight-Loving trail, and the sounds of crickets in the long grass and the dry croak of frogs beside the well. It was companionable and familiar, and vaguely sad for reasons I could not put my finger on, reminiscent of some other time altogether.

I wondered then if we might quite possibly be the very last of our kind.

CHAPTER FOUR

I TELEPHONED the sheriff while I drank my morning's first cup of coffee on the gallery. I lit a cigarette and listened to the cattle begin to stir in the confines of the paddock down below, while I paced the short distance allowed me by the tether of the coiled cord that stretched all the way through the gap in the screen door.

The morning had arrived in shades of turquoise, cold and clear, and the morning star continued to shine long after the sun had topped the ridgeline. A thin layer of cloud cover lay off to the west, and I felt the portent of afternoon rain.

"Who was that?" Jesse asked as she came into the kitchen. She was dressed in blue jeans and T-shirt, and wrapped in a thick woolen Indian-print sweater.

"I'm meeting with Lloyd Skadden this afternoon."

She stirred cream into her coffee and leaned a hip against the kitchen counter.

"Here?"

"No," I said. "At his office."

"All the way up there? He knows the Works have started, right?"

"He is aware of that. But he said he had some things to talk to me about."

"Besides our rustled cattle?"

"Apparently."

Jesse placed her spoon in the sink and blew at the steam that rose from her cup. "About what, then?"

"No idea," I said. "But he did not want to talk about it on the phone."

"He'd better not be trying to hustle you for a campaign contribution."

"He's a political animal. I don't think he even knows when he's doing it."

I kissed her on the cheek, stepped over to the percolator, and poured myself another cup.

"Don't worry about me," I smiled. "I did not just fall here from space."

———

THE DRIVE to Lewiston took nearly two hours in good weather, along a winding two-lane that had been cut into the floor of a narrow valley that ran the entire length of the county. Steep ridges rose up on either side, where the last vestiges of snow lay melting among the scree and deadfall in the shadows of glaciated stone.

Lloyd Skadden was only the third full-time sheriff in the history of Meriwether County. Fifteen years ago, the whole region could be effectively policed by a shopkeeper cop whose main activity centered around breaking up fistfights at the Bristo when the hired hands turned loose the last of their paychecks on rye whisky, glasses of beer, and a spin around the dance floor with local girls who lacked either the means or motivation to leave town and seek more promising prospects. The completion of the interstate several miles to the west of us had pretty much left our lives untouched, with the exception of the improvements it precipitated in the way we transported our stock. And even though some municipalities along its route had experienced noticeable growth, our entire county still consisted of just two towns: Lewiston, the county seat to the north; and Meridian in the south, nearest my ranch. We remained an unincorporated area isolated both by geography and the unreliable road system that served our more rural backcountry, with a livestock population that far exceeded that of humans, and we tended to like it that way.

A light sprinkle of rain began to fall on my windshield as I finally reached the stoplight that marked my arrival in Lewiston. A serpentine wall made of mortar and stone was decorated with the various insignia of service clubs and fraternal organizations, and the name of the town in large block letters that had gone to green with the patina of age and weather.

I parked in the lot next to the municipal building, got out, and pulled down the brim of my hat against the mounting rainfall. A hand-painted sign on the glass doors directed me down a hallway that was lit by the flutter of fluorescent tubing and smelled of mildew and trapped heat, and dead-ended at the door to the office of the county sheriff.

The receptionist inside was brusque, officious, and at least forty-five pounds overweight. Her pinched features and facial expression suggested she was a person whose life had been defined by a long series of disappointments and personal humiliation, and was happy for every opportunity to return them in kind.

Lloyd Skadden intercepted me before I had the chance to announce myself.

"Sorry to make you drive all the way up here, Ty," he said, and led the way into his office.

His hair was oiled and brushed straight back from a deeply lined forehead, his complexion ruddy with permanent white circles that raccooned his eyes where sunglasses had protected them from the elements.

He gestured me toward a guest chair while he took up his position behind a desk of dark walnut that had been elaborately adorned with the hand-carved images of elk, deer, and caribou. Behind him, the gold-fringed flags of the United States of America and the County of Meriwether hung limp on their stands at either side of a matching credenza, and bookended a framed collection of shoulder patches that had been gifted to him by other law enforcement agencies.

"Sal, bring Mr. Dawson some coffee, will you, sweetheart?" he called through the doorway, then turned his attention to me. "So, tell me about your cattle problem."

Lloyd Skadden was not a large man in conventional terms, but his carriage and personal boldness created an impression of authority and influence that was at odds with both his physical stature and the man I knew him to be. Like mine, his family had helped settle this valley and had earned itself a certain amount of respect in prior generations. But the intricacies of land ownership and ranching had not come naturally to Lloyd's father, and that deficiency had taken its toll on the architecture and direction of Lloyd Skadden's life. In his eyes, I imagined I could still see the young man he had once been: swilling beer in the backseats of jacked-up automobiles and tossing the empties on the unpaved shoulders of dark rural roads, shooting holes in the signs that marked blind curves and deer crossings, or making vulgar and demeaning remarks to adolescent girls as they stood in shy clusters outside the minimart. Still, I did not actually know him well enough to dislike him outright, had in fact contributed small amounts to his campaigns for office over the years, and I prayed that I was judging him too harshly.

"I've lost a bull and three breeding cows in the past few weeks," I said. "And three more, from what I understand, over on the Corcoran lease."

"Don't let that old coot wind you up, Dawson. He's old as the hills. I'm pretty sure he was around when the Columbia was just a trickle."

"I buried most of them myself, Sheriff—"

"Call me 'Lloyd'," he said.

A sudden gust of wind drove a torrent of rain against the window that sounded like bird shot ticking on the glass.

"These animals were not simply butchered for meat. Half of them were nothing more than a pink stain on a crater by the time I found them."

He looked at me quizzically.

"You saying somebody blew them up?"

"I only know what I've seen. It's why I called you. I need your help to track the sonofabitch who's doing harm to my animals."

Skadden leaned back in his leather chair and stared out into the storm, while he pulled together the filaments of thought inside his head. He puffed his cheeks and heaved a long sigh as he turned to face me again.

"There's a reason I asked you here today, Ty. Fact is, I don't have the resources to be your stock detective. I don't have the resources to do that for anybody at the moment."

The receptionist stalked into the room with a pot of freshly brewed coffee, cream and sugar, and a pair of ceramic mugs. She wordlessly sat one mug in front of me and poured without making eye contact with either of us, then placed the tray on the credenza.

"Thank you, Sal," he said to her retreating back. "And please close the door behind you."

I cupped the coffee between my palms, absorbing the heat while I waited for the door strike to snap shut.

"Sheriff—"

"I need you to listen to me for a minute, Ty," he interrupted. "I mentioned that I had a reason for asking you to come all the way up here, and here it is: We've got a problem. Possibly a big problem. You've been following what's going on over at Pine Ridge?"

Anyone with a television set or a car radio had been hearing about little else, apart from the daily reports out of the Senate Watergate Committee describing unimaginable behavior coming from the White House. The toothpaste was coming out of the tube, and wasn't going to slide back in. Even so, I had no idea what the siege at Wounded Knee had to do with me, or with the president's growing troubles, and I set my coffee mug on his desk, preparing to direct our conversation back to my cattle problem.

He preempted any comment by showing me the palm of his hand.

"Just give me a minute here," he said. "About six weeks ago, 200 Sioux agitators showed up out of nowhere and took that whole town hostage. A whole damn *town*."

"I am aware of that—"

"*Yesterday*, some fella with an airplane went and dropped a ton of food down out of the sky for those Indians. The feds, dumb asses that they are, opened fire when the natives came out to pick that crap up off the ground, and managed to shoot an Indian in the head. TV news cameras got the whole damn thing on film."

He stopped and waited for me to absorb the weight of his words, interlacing the fingers of hands that were dusted with freckles and a pattern of white scars left behind by something other than manual labor.

"Thing is, it's turning into a war zone over there, Ty, and there's nothing that says it can't happen here. The wheels are coming off this whole damn country."

I did not follow his leap in logic, and it showed on my face.

He drew a deep breath and refocused.

"I received a call yesterday. Some woman down south of you is stirring up all kinds of dust about the BLM rounding up wild mustangs for slaughter. Now, I've put a call in, but haven't heard back whether there's any truth to that or not. But I can say this: when the media gets a hold of a story like that, the circus comes to town. I'm not talking about a little sideshow here—I'm talking about a Woodstock-sized hippie fest that we are in no position to handle."

"I think you might be getting ahead of yourself," I said.

"Listen, I'm smart enough not to borrow trouble. I learned that a long time ago. But that's not all of it. You've heard of the Charlatans?"

"The motorcycle club."

"It's not a club, it's a gang. They make a pile of money running dope and shaking down small businesses. Three weeks ago, they skinned a man alive with a carrot peeler. That happened down in Fresno."

"Okay."

"In Sacramento, they gang raped a mentally retarded girl. She uses a wheelchair now."

"*Okay*," I said. "I get it. What about them?"

"They're coming this way."

"Because of some wild mustangs? I'm sorry, but that sounds a bit hard to believe."

He waved a hand in the air and looked at me as though I were a slow child.

"Easter's less than a week away, Dawson," he said. "These jokers have planned some kind of rally that's going to bring a whole mess of 'em straight up the interstate and right through our county on their way somewhere up north. And *that* little bit of intel comes straight from the feds."

He pointed a stubby finger at me for emphasis.

"You mix that bunch in with a gathering of horse-huggers, hippies, and news cameras, you have got yourself a perfect storm. And I will not have our towns held hostage like those folks in South Dakota."

I took a sip of coffee and scanned the room as I processed what he was telling me. For all the things that Lloyd Skadden was and was not, I had not ever known him to be a reactionary, and he appeared to me to be genuinely worked up. My eyes landed on a framed photo of the sheriff swapping smiles with John Dean and Richard Nixon, which apparently had been snapped at a campaign event during happier times for all of them.

"Sheriff, I understand your concerns. But I don't know why you're telling me all of this," I said. "Or what it has to do with my dead cattle."

His face flushed and accentuated the tangle of broken capillaries on his cheeks.

"I am asking for your help, Dawson," he said.

He had a vaguely garbled manner of speech that put me in mind of a man who spoke while chewing food.

"I don't understand that statement," I said.

"You are a stiff-necked sonofabitch, aren't you?"

"Excuse me?"

He stood and began pacing behind his ornamented desk. His eyes were glued to the carpet as he spoke.

"I have a geography problem here. I can't look after both ends of this county at the same time. Those bikers and all the other riff-raff can set one town on fire while they rape and ransack the other: a bait-and-switch. I got close to 4,000 souls here in Lewiston who are counting on me to keep them safe."

"You've got another couple thousand in Meridian, Sheriff. I suspect they'd like to be safe too."

He smiled and turned on his heel.

"It appears that you are hearing me now."

At first I was incredulous. Then I got angry.

"You want me to act on your behalf in Meridian?" I said. "There's not a chance in hell I'd do that."

"I intend to appoint you as my undersheriff for the south end of the county, with my full authority, to act as a law enforcement officer. And to deputize additional help if you need it."

"I'm sorry, Lloyd, but that's not going to happen. I'm not the man for the job."

"Don't try to hooraw me, Ty Dawson. You are exactly the man for the job. I am aware of your service with the military police."

"That was a long time ago."

"Time don't matter, this'll be like riding a bike. And age don't matter either. I must have a good ten years on you—I'm coming up on fifty-some and it don't keep me from kicking ass when the situation calls for it."

"I'm a rancher, Lloyd."

His face went red again, and I knew the conversation was getting away from me.

"You are a *man*, goddammit, and Meriwether County needs you."

He slid his hands into the pockets of his trousers and resumed pacing, which appeared to calm him down.

"I'm not asking you to kiss me on the lips here, Ty. We ain't getting married. I need you to watch this county's back door while I mind the front. Just 'til this situation blows by. After that, you can go back to the ranch, and we can all get back to your rustling problem."

I had always considered myself to be a reasonable and responsible man, and I had to admit that he was making a practical point. If he was wrong about all of it, no real harm will have been done, other than taking me away from the ranch for a few days.

"What are we talking about here, time-wise?" I said. "I just got my Spring Works underway."

"You got men for that."

I felt my face get hot again.

"With respect, Lloyd," I said evenly. "*You've* got men for what you're asking of me. And I don't appreciate people telling me how to operate my business."

He surprised me when he laughed out loud.

"Ty, what I got is me plus two other deputies. Three, if you count Myron, which nobody usually does 'cause he's a dipshit."

"Myron's your son."

"Myron is my second ex-wife's son, and he don't have the sense to smoke a cigarette from the end that ain't on fire. That aside, four men are not enough to cover a county this size twenty-four hours a day. That's a fact, and you know it."

"You didn't answer my question."

He pursed his lips and looked out the window again. The downpour had slowed to a drizzle again, and a chain of sun breaks was dappling the face of the mountain.

"A week. Two weeks tops. If this thing turns out to be a snipe hunt, we're done. And if it really turns to shit, then we got a problem that'll probably require the National Guard."

"I'm going to have to think on it," I said.

"Listen, Ty. I didn't want to have to bring this up, but have you ever heard of a thing called Posse Comitatus? I'll save you the trouble of looking it up. It's a statute that says I can press you into service whether you like it or not. Don't dig your heels and make me do that."

"I don't respond well to threats," I said.

"That wasn't a threat. That was a recitation of the law. If I want to conscript you, I can. I would prefer it, though, if you perceived it as your civic obligation—like jury duty—and you're the man to get it done."

"Keep blowing sunshine up my ass, I'm liable to combust."

"It ain't sunshine, Ty," he said, his tone mirroring sincerity. "If I thought there was a better man for the job, I'd be talking to him, not you."

———∽∽∽———

DUSK WAS falling by the time I pulled the truck to a stop in the pea-gravel lot beside the house.

The sky had turned gunmetal gray, but the clouds glowed pink and the air smelled of applewood and the chimney smoke that rose up from the bunkhouse. Yellow light spilled from the window over the kitchen sink, and should have looked warm and domestic and inviting. Instead, I steeled myself for the conversation I was about to have with Jesse.

It did not go exactly as I had planned it during my long drive home.

"Are you out of your goddamned mind?" I believe were the first words she said once I had finished.

CHAPTER FIVE

I WAS PUSHING bacon around the skillet on the stove, barely tasting my coffee when the telephone rang. I moved the pan off the fire and stepped over to answer it.

"Hi, Daddy," my daughter said, and my pulse rate jumped a little, the way it always did when I heard my girl's voice.

"Hello, Cricket." I smiled into the phone. "Pretty early in the morning, isn't it?"

Her given name was Laura, after my mother, but she'd been Cricket to me ever since she had taken her first baby steps. She had a way of crawl-hopping when she started to figure out how to walk, and the nickname stuck. She was nineteen now, and nearing the end of her sophomore year of college in Colorado. She was Jesse's and my only child and the love of my life; she's smart, and she's pretty and I worry about her every day of my life.

"I was raised on a ranch, remember?" she said.

There was noise on her end of the line that sounded like highway traffic.

"What's all that racket?" I asked. "Where are you?"

"I'm calling from a pay phone. Where's Mom? Is she around?"

My heart fell, though I told myself it shouldn't. Ever since my daughter had gone off to school, her relationship with me had changed, dissolving into a pattern of faltering conversations punctuated by fits and false-starts and missteps. It seemed that nearly every time we spoke anymore, we'd end up mired in talk of politics, injustice, or the sins of the Establishment, my choices of words usually the wrong ones.

"She's still in bed," I said.

Cricket was silent for a moment too long, and the hiss of air brakes from an eighteen-wheeler spun down the line at me. I heard her sigh.

I felt like that kid in the comic strip who tries to kick a football that gets pulled away from him at the last moment. He falls for it every time.

"You still there?" I asked.

"I'm still here. Listen, Dad, I was hoping I could come home for spring break. You think that would be okay?"

"Of course it's okay. I'll send you a plane ticket. Just tell me what day you want to come."

She covered the mouthpiece and spoke to someone in words I couldn't hear.

"Don't worry about it," she said. "I'll drive out instead."

"That sounds—"

"I've gotta go, Dad. Tell Mom I love her, and I'll call back a little later to fill in the details."

"I love you, Cricket."

"You too," she said, and the line went dead.

———

I HAD lost any interest in breakfast, so I drained the bacon grease from the frying pan, refilled my coffee mug, and walked down to the office instead.

Sunrise was still half an hour away, but the waxwings and thrush were already stirring in the trees and the air was laced with moss and sloughed pine needles. A smattering of stars still flickered in the predawn and a breeze blew down from the eastern slopes that frosted my breath into vaporous silver clouds as I picked my way down the path between the conifers toward the dim halo of yellow light from a fixture mounted outside the office door.

I lit a fire in the woodstove, warmed my outstretched palms as the flames took hold, and watched threads of gray smoke float by outside the window. I glanced at the feedstore calendar tacked to the wall and hung my hat on the coatrack. I took a seat in a rolling chair behind one of the two matching Steelcase desks that occupied the center of the narrow room and stared out the window while I finished my coffee, my boots propped on the writing surface.

False dawn had given way to the real thing, and the leaves and blossoms on the dogwoods outside were shimmering, reflecting daybreak, when Caleb Wheeler pushed into the office.

"Didn't expect to find you here," he said. He strode to the woodstove to warm his backside. "You brew any coffee?"

I showed him my empty mug and shook my head.

"Brought this from the house."

"I'll do it." He kept his heavy coat on while he spooned coffee grounds from a can into the percolator. "You know, for a smart man, you can sure be a dumb sonofabitch."

"You heard?"

"Of course I heard."

"Let me guess," I said. "Lankard Downing."

"Where else does news come from in this town?"

Wheeler shrugged out of his coat, hung it on the hook beside my hat, and sat down at the desk that faced mine. He shot a glance at the coffee pot and turned his stare back at me.

Lankard Downing owned a bar in Meridian called the Cottonwood Blossom that was favored by ranch hands and the occasional tourist in search of a glimpse of authentic Western life along the back roads of cow country. Downing was a consumptive-looking septuagenarian with hollow cheeks and face like the chipped edge of a hatchet who took pleasure in sharing stories that usually involved the misfortunes of others. He did not disseminate news as a community service, it was a character flaw. If bad news traveled fast in this part of the county, it was largely because of him.

"What the hell's the matter with you anyway?" Wheeler asked.

"Lloyd Skadden convinced me it's a thing that needs doing. Mostly convinced me."

"And what is 'mostly' supposed to mean?"

"I came down here for some peace and quiet, Caleb."

"You came to the wrong damned place for that," he sighed. His knees popped as he hauled himself out of his chair to get his coffee. "At least we got some good hands this season. I guess we won't miss you for a week or two."

"You have any problems, let Jesse know."

"I intend to. At least she ain't as stubborn as you, and probably twice as smart."

I smiled to myself, thought my foreman must be mellowing. He'd usually rather pass a kidney stone than pay someone a compliment.

"Probably," I said.

The sun broke through the trees and came streaming in between the jalousies, painting rectangular patterns on the floor.

———

I MADE a left off the county two-lane onto a narrow dirt road whose entrance was virtually obscured from view by a cluster of white oak and cascara. A young couple ate sliced watermelon at a table fashioned from reclaimed planks balanced between twin stacks of apple crates that had been placed in front of an open air fruit stand. They smiled as I passed and flashed me a peace sign.

I eased my pickup around loose stones and deep potholes that were still brimming with mud-colored runoff, following a road that opened on one side to acres of unbounded agricultural land that bore the appearance of decades of abandonment and neglect. The other was bordered by low hills that arose from the flats and a fence made from strands of steel wire that had been stretched between posts fringed with overgrown tufts of brown grass. No Trespassing signs were streaked with rust where they had been fastened to the fencing with crimped iron hooks, and creaked as they swayed in the gusts that moved down the arroyos.

I crested a long sloping rise in the road and had my first look at the homestead that belonged to Teresa Pineu. I pulled to a stop, grabbed a pair of field glasses from my glove compartment, and stood beside the open door of my truck.

Her home had been crafted from the carcass of a doublewide that had been mounted on a foundation of concrete block and surrounded by an apron of garden lattice that had once been painted white. A short set of stairs led to a porch landing where the front door was tied open with a knotted rope and a length of curtain fabric fell out through a side window and was fluttering in the wind.

A goat, tied to a metal post with what appeared to be a length of clothesline, was chewing a piece of rotted fruit and pissing a hole in the dirt while a pair of naked toddlers roamed around nearby in search of something in the weeds.

I saw no sign of Teresa Pineu, but her place was now surrounded by a makeshift encampment of lean-tos, tents, and pop-up campers and populated by no fewer than one hundred people. An American flag flew upside down from a pole fixed to a multicolored school bus where a cluster of people had gathered themselves into a circle and danced to the rhythm of drums made from upturned plastic feed buckets and rusted metal cans.

I dropped the binoculars from my eyes, returned them to the glove box, and drove slowly down the hill. I parked between Teresa's place and a drainage ditch overgrown with disfigured shrubs and dead brush that ran behind a tar-paper building with a door made of corrugated metal. When I stepped down from the truck the only sounds I could hear were the incessant banging of that metal door and the yapping of a dog from the encampment. The drums had gone silent and I felt the convergence of 200 eyeballs focused on the back of my neck.

I used to have dreams about the war, the savage battle at Chipyong-ni and the evacuation of Seoul. I hold no illusions that my dreams were any worse than those suffered by untold numbers of veterans returning from the field of battle. When I awoke from those nightmares, though, no matter the hour or the state of the weather, I would dress and walk down to the barn and curry the horses, or study the work that had stacked up on my desk. The frequency of the nightmares has subsided over the years, but the images remain deeply embedded in some neglected place together with the visceral recall of that thing some call muscle memory.

It had been my intention to make this a low-key visit, but present circumstances appeared to have scotched that plan. I strode toward the front door of Teresa Pineu's trailer, and hand-checked the pistol strapped into the holster concealed beneath the three-quarter duster I wore. I wasn't expecting violence, but experience had taught me that's when it most often occurred.

I made it nearly halfway to the foot of the stairs when I caught the approach of two men coming up on my flank in my peripheral vision. They were dressed nearly identically in faded denim jeans, lace-up steel-toed boots, and the familiar leather vests with sewn-on patches favored by outlaw motor- cycle gangs. The man taking the lead was the taller of the two, with dark brown hair that hung beyond his shoulders, and a narrow, leporine face that was oily with perspiration, and a mustache whose ends grew all the way to his jawline. The other one was shorter, but broader across the chest, and wore a full Garibaldi beard that gave him the appearance of a lumberjack. This one's cheeks were scarred and pitted where they showed above his facial hair, and his bovine eyes looked like pools of stagnant water. They made an odd pair, but then I looked at the crowd around me and thought, *com- pared to what?*

They took up a position between me and Teresa Pineu's trailer, stood shoulder to shoulder, and waited for me.

"Help you with something?" the Rabbit said.

His clothes smelled of asphalt and tar and his own ali- mentary odors.

"I doubt it," I said. "I'm here to see Ms. Pineu."

"Not today, cowboy," he said. "Turn it around and go home."

They possessed the eyes of predators and men who took their pleasure from defiling and abusing the weakest of the herd while masquerading as their protectors.

I eyed each one in turn, then swiveled my head to gauge the mood of the mob behind me. I saw that we had been joined by a second pair of young men by then, one with a movie camera balanced on his shoulder, who stood off to one side, maintaining a safe distance.

I looked in the direction of the newcomers and said, "I'm not making any comments for the news."

"We're not the news," the one without the camera said, and tried to charm me with a smile. "We're filming a documentary." Then he hooked a thumb over his shoulder, indicating a commercial van whose sides were painted with a local network logo that I hadn't noticed before. "Those guys are the news."

"Thanks for the clarification," I said. "My earlier statement applies to all of you."

I stepped in close to the bikers and spoke softly.

"I've long believed that the decisions that end up having the deepest impact on our lives nearly always seem of little consequence at the time. Know what I mean?"

The Bovine pressed an elbow into the Rabbit's arm and showed me a feral smile. "You believe this guy?"

Rabbit cast his eyes to the ground that separated us, and widened his stance. The inside of my head suddenly felt like the scorched floor of a desert landscape strewn with thornbushes. It was an old but familiar sensation that accompanied dark and violent behavior.

"You do not want to act on the thoughts you've got in your head right now," I said.

"And *you* don't speak to me that way, cowboy. You think I'm some kind of bitch?"

"Maybe," I shrugged. "I don't know you yet."

I knew what he was about to do, and he didn't disappoint me. He made a move for the hunting knife that hung from a scabbard on his belt, but I was quicker, and had my pistol aimed squarely at his eye socket, hammer cocked and ready, before his hand reached the hilt of his blade.

"You ever try to pig-stick me, you greasy fuck, you'd better do it quicker than that. Step out of my way now, both of you, or they'll be peeling you off the wall with a paint scraper."

His pupils spun down to pinpricks, and he looked like a mental patient trying to comprehend his own illness.

Teresa Pineu stepped out onto the elevated porch of her trailer, crossed her arms, and studied us.

"That's enough," she said finally. "Come on up, Mr. Dawson."

I stepped around the bikers as I holstered my weapon and ascended the stairs.

Teresa made a dismissive gesture in the general direction of the crowd and called out, "Go on back to whatever you were doing. Everything's fine."

We stood together on the porch and watched the throng begin to disperse. The bikers tried to mad dog me with their eyes.

"Keep the shiny side up, fellas," I said, and touched my fingers to my hat brim.

———

TERESA PINEU was a woman who kept mostly to herself and about whom I knew very little, apart from the nodding acquaintance we'd developed over the years in the fulfillment of our daily activities. Meridian is a very small town.

She was unusually attractive, nearly six feet tall and fit. I guessed her to be somewhere approaching her late forties, but she still possessed a youthful olive complexion, and the mahogany hair and fawn-colored eyes that spoke of a Mediterranean heritage. Teresa had earned a reputation as one of the finest horse trainers in the state, and a passionate advocate for indigenous wildlife. She had built a living, as had I, out of the responsibility for the care of other lives—a dedication and fidelity that is alien to those who do not work or live with animals.

We stood in the sunshine on her porch, looking out over the odd conglomeration of people who had responded to Teresa's public outcry regarding the roundup of wild mustangs on the BLM property that shared a border with her own. My gaze landed on a girl with wild curls of blond hair and an armband made of colored beads, dipping a wand into a jar and blowing soap bubbles into the wind.

"So, did Sheriff Skadden send you all the way down here to shut me up?" she asked me.

"No, ma'am. As far as I'm concerned, this is still America, and this is your property, and you've got the right to say whatever you want."

She studied my face for a long moment, looking for some sign of duplicity, and finding none.

"Are you familiar with the verses of the Bible that pertain to man's dominion over animals?"

"I'm pretty sure I am," I said.

"Are you familiar with Ecclesiastes?"

"Can you be more specific?"

She leaned her elbows on the railing and gazed into the rolling pastureland beyond the wire fence.

"'For what happens to the children of man and what happens to the beasts is the same; as one dies, so dies the other. They all have the same breath, and man has no advantage over the beasts, for all is vanity.'"

She turned to face me before she continued.

"Do you know that verse?" she asked.

"It has a ring to it."

"I believe that the dimensions of that statement are simple, and need to be taken seriously."

"I don't disagree with that outlook, Ms. Pineu," I said. "But it's these people who are becoming a cause of concern for the sheriff."

She pursed her lips and a flush of color came into her cheeks.

"Mr. Dawson," she said. "My life has taught me that any statement that precedes the word 'but' doesn't count."

"Let me put it bluntly: the presence of those bikers should cause you some alarm. Because those two idiots are only the beginning. I've been led to believe that many more just like them are on their way. These are volatile, violent, and dangerous men."

"They perceived you as a threat to me," she said.

"They perceived me as a threat to their authority, and their ability to run roughshod over the others who have come here to support you. They will use all of you for their own purposes, and they have the capacity and potential to bring a great deal of suffering to everybody here. They were about to plant a bowie knife between my ribs."

"So you *are* here to shut me up."

"No, ma'am, I truly am not. I am sympathetic to your cause. But this situation could turn ugly."

"Like Wounded Knee?"

"I sincerely hope not."

"I think Russell Means has got his hands full, Mr. Dawson."

"I wish you'd consider a different method, is all I'm trying to tell you," I said. "You've already got a news crew parked outside. Once this hits the airwaves, you're going to lose control."

"Let me ask you something," she said. "Is the murder of hundreds of feral horses okay with you?"

"I've already spoken to Melissa Vernon at the bureau. The BLM claims to be offering them for adoption."

"That's bullshit, and you know it. The Wild Horse Act, that's bullshit, too. They'll call it 'adoption,' or they'll call it an 'auction,' but either way it ends the same. Private contractors bid on the animals and sell them off to meat-packing plants. There's not a thing the BLM can do to stop it either. They're *complicit* in it, for chrissakes."

"I'm not here to tell you that you're wrong," I said. "I'm here to encourage you to disperse this crowd. If you don't, it's going to get bigger. And if that happens, it's going to get dangerous. For everybody, for the whole county. I'm sure you can see the potential for that."

"It's already dangerous to the whole damn county," she said, the whites of her eyes shot through with red and shining wet with rage. "You can give this message to Melissa Vernon at the bureau for me: When they stop, I'll stop. Until then, I intend to exercise my First Amendment right to say and do whatever the hell I damn well please."

AFTER DINNER that night, I sat on the porch swing in the cool evening air and smoked a cigarette in the light of a single candle Jesse had placed on the table inside a frosted glass hurricane cover.

I did not discuss my meeting with Teresa Pineu, though I knew that Jesse was worried by my silence. I do not take solace in talking about things that trouble me. I find no comfort in sharing my pain. Instead, I hold out in gray silence and hope that solutions will present themselves so that when I finally do speak of them, they will have an ending and not mere ellipsis.

I listened to the distant vibration of frogs as they croaked along the creek bed and the sound of night birds in the tall timber, and crushed my spent cigarette in the ashtray when I heard the screen door open.

Jesse stepped outside and sat beside me on the swing bench with a container of chocolate chip ice cream and a spoon. I thought about my father, and watching him braid a lariat out of horsehair on this very same spot. He had come from a time that required little justification for action, and had shown me how nature encouraged the strong to live while the weak were allowed to die. This was not modern thinking, and those lines did not seem to be cut quite as straight these days.

"My grandfather once told me that before he moved out here, he worked for an old man named Patch who owned a slaughterhouse back in Kansas," I said. "He told me the man killed the cattle for their hides and tallow, but he'd throw the meat to the hogs."

"I wish I could take memories like that one right out of your skull," Jesse said.

"He told me they'd do almost 200 head a day like that."

She slid the spoon into the ice cream container and placed them on the floor. She leaned her head against my shoulder and stared out to the darkness.

"I've been trying to keep my disappointments to myself, but it hasn't been doing too much good," I told her.

"I'm sorry for what I said to you before," she said. "You're not out of your mind."

I kissed her on the forehead and we sat together in the silence until the candle on the table began to smoke, guttering in its own melted wax. I stood and gave the pedestal a quarter turn, righted the wick, and blew it out. And then we went to bed.

PART TWO:
SHOTGUN MESSENGER

CHAPTER SIX

I AWOKE FROM a restless and dream-littered sleep feeling like someone had hammered a half-dozen Capewell nails into my forehead.

I eased myself out of bed and dressed as quietly as I could, careful not to disturb the soft rhythm of Jesse's breath. I parted the curtains on the bedroom window and peered outside into the ink-black stillness of predawn, then let them fall back into place before I padded out of the room in stocking feet and closed the door gently behind me.

Wyatt came out of his bed and watched as I took a jar of instant coffee from the pantry, scooped a couple spoonfuls into a mug, and pushed my feet into my boots. He sat quietly beside me while I scratched his head and waited for the teapot on the burner to come to a boil. The only sounds in the house came from the flutter of blue flame on the stove, the ticking of the mantel clock, and the echo of voices inside my head that followed me out of my dreams.

A few minutes later I dumped the remains of bitter coffee into the sink, buttoned myself into a sheepskin coat, slipped on a pair of gloves, and went out into the cold morning with Wyatt close behind me at my heels.

I slid between the wood-fence railings and crouched low to hunt the shadows of the horses inside the corral, their clouds of breath like frozen smoke against the sky. I located my favorite stock horse, a young bay Morgan named Drambuie that I just called Boo. I allowed him to see the halter and lead that dangled from my hand, and he snorted and blew in anticipation. Wyatt paced outside the gate, wagging expectantly while I slipped the halter into place, buckled the crown behind Boo's ears, and led him up the hill toward the tack room.

The air around me smelled of horseflesh and freshly churned soil and the sweet alluvial scent of the creek bed, and I saw a light flicker on in the bunkhouse. A trace of silver smoke rose from the chimney, and I stepped into the stirrups, settled myself into the cantle, and gigged the bay forward with Wyatt close on my flank.

———

THE HOLLOW call of an owl cascaded from somewhere inside the tall timber, and the foliage was alive with the whistling of crickets as I dismounted and tied the horse off to a hitch post near the gate at the family plot. I drew a rag from the back pocket of my jeans, and wiped dust and dried mud off the stones that marked the resting places for two generations of Dawsons. I sat on my haunches beside my father's headstone and listened for answers, idly watching a single sodium light blink from the top of a radio tower that was perched on the ridge at the far end of the valley, a distant and solitary candle. I sat there for nearly an hour, until the outline of the mountain came into focus against the pale blue backdrop of sunrise. I found myself visiting more frequently these days, in search of the wisdom I had so often dismissed as a younger man, and I knew that my forebears would find some irony in that.

Boo pawed the soil as I remounted and turned him toward the summit of the hill. Every now and then from here, when the wind blew just right, I could hear the muffled drone of the interstate miles away, or the growl of an eighteen-wheeler downshifting in preparation for its climb along the grade. I could not see the highway, buried deep between the folds of the canyon, but I could hear it very faintly. And it sounded as alien and unwelcome to me as had the thundering hoofbeats of the Mongol hordes when they swept across the steppes in the conquest of Qara Khitai.

—————

THE FULL flush of morning had broken across the open range and grassland by the time I reached the trailhead to the path that would lead me back to the ranch. I was about halfway down the slope when I spotted a lone rider walking his horse in my direction. I recognized the blue roan gelding as one of mine, and knew the rider must be Dub Naylor.

Wyatt continued to work the open field, looking for something to do while Dub brought his horse up beside me and reined him to a stop.

"Morning, boss," he said.

A wide smile accentuated the creases in his sun-weathered skin, and he reached into the pocket of his shirt and withdrew a container of snuff.

"Dub," I said. "What brings you out here all by yourself?"

The cowboy had earned a reputation as a world-class single-handed talker, so I was not entirely surprised that my foreman had sent him out alone. My other men seemed to treat it as a form of punishment to spend a whole day in the saddle with him. Nevertheless, Dub Naylor was one of the best itinerant cowhands who ever unkinked a rope.

"Old Caleb sent me up to the North Camp to drag back the strays," he said, then packed a pinch of snuff into the hollow of his bottom lip. He sealed the lid back on the can and slipped it back into his pocket.

"Tell you what," I said. "Why don't you take Wyatt up there with you? He's restless for a little work."

I didn't think the dog would mind the chatter. I whistled to Wyatt and motioned for him to follow Dub, and clucked my horse forward before a conversation could take hold.

"You'd better jump some gully, Dub. You got a ways to go."

Dub rode off in the direction I had just come from and I heard him singing to himself as he disappeared into the trees, with Wyatt close behind.

"I swear, Boo," I said to my horse as I leaned forward and patted him on the neck. "I think that man might just up and die if it ever got too quiet."

IN THE twenty-four hours that had passed since my previous visit to Teresa Pineu, the campsite had bloated to at least three times its former size, and had sprawled onto the neighboring fallow farmland. In addition to the documentary filmmakers and the single local news crew from before, the networks had sent backup: two news trucks, emblazoned on their sides with call letters and logos—one had come from Salem, the other all the way down from Portland. If the atmosphere had been merely disorganized before, it was approaching anarchic now.

I'd parked my truck in a dry ditch at the side of the road, some distance up from the entrance to Teresa's property. Cars, pickups, and camper vans of every description and state of repair lined the roadway and had only left room for access on foot.

When I finally passed between her gateposts and stepped across the cattle guard, I spotted Teresa Pineu standing at the center of a ring of journalists, speaking into microphones affixed to shiny chrome booms while the cameras recorded it all. She was making broad sweeping gestures in the direction of the BLM land on the other side of her fence as she spoke, though I only caught the tail end of her statement.

"Here's a little history lesson: The Bureau of Land Management was originally established to survey land so that it could be sold off to private citizens for subsequent settlement, to parcel out the land grants that had been promised to war veterans and to homesteaders who were willing to risk everything they had in the unsettled territories.

"The bureau has since changed its mission, and now controls huge tracts of land that exceed 50 percent of this entire state; more than 60 percent of Idaho; and over 70 percent of Nevada. And that's only the beginning."

I pressed my way gently through the crowd that surrounded the makeshift news conference and stood at the edge of the congregation. Their collective presence formed a pungent cloud that smelled of unwashed bodies, tobacco, patchouli oil, and marijuana smoke.

"All I am asking is this," Teresa said. "What the hell gives them the right to round up wild animals that have been roaming these mountains for generations, and sell them off for commercial slaughter? Did *you* give them that power?"

Teresa Pineu had done a masterful job of riling her audience, and while she did not have the temerity to reveal the smile I was sure she held at bay, the upward tilt of her chin and the tight line of her lips betrayed the satisfaction she felt when the assembly shouted their answer in unison.

"No!"

"Did *I* give them that power?" she appended.

"No!"

"Thank you," she said and took a moment to give each camera lens a usable shot of her face. "That's all I have at this time."

The news people shouted questions at her as she walked slowly back to her trailer, but she ignored them. I started to follow her, but someone took hold of my arm.

"Excuse me, Sheriff."

It was one of the documentary boys I had seen before, and he had his camera lens pointed six inches from my face.

"Please step back," I said. "And I'm not the sheriff."

"That's not what we've been told," he persisted.

His face was a mask of earnestness and youthful ardor that struck me as admirable, naive, and misguided all at once. He couldn't have been twenty-two or –three, and wore an uncombed mop of blond hair that fell past his ears, wide sideburns that grew to his jawline, and a necklace fashioned from brown beads that circled his neck like a garrote.

"I am the temporary undersheriff for the southern portion of Meriwether County, and I would appreciate it if you would step away from me and allow me to do my job."

"Are you here to arrest Teresa Pineu?"

"I don't have any interest in arresting anybody at the moment. Except maybe you, if you don't let go of my arm."

On horseback, I still felt like a young and able hand. But here on the ground I felt like I carried the weight of every single year I'd tallied, and the phantom pain of every fall I'd landed from the back of an unbroken colt or the kicks I'd absorbed hog-tying calves. Still I had to reluctantly admit that Lloyd Skadden had been right about two things: this present situation was rapidly approaching the threshold of outright chaos; and my enforcement of the law, together with the cynical view of the world that accompanied it, was proving to be very much like riding a bike.

The young filmmaker turned loose of me, but kept the camera pressed into my space.

"Can I just get a statement from you?"

"I don't give statements," I said. "Make an appointment with Sheriff Skadden up in Lewiston."

"But—"

"I'm finished here." I heard the incessant hum of the camera's motors pushing film stock even as I walked away.

Teresa Pineu was seated on an L-shaped sofa tucked into the corner of her living room, arms outstretched along the back and looking very pleased with herself. An open bottle of Hires Root Beer was sweating beads of condensation onto a paper napkin on the table in front of her while a vent from a roof-mounted swamp cooler blew a stream of tepid air into the room.

"Close the door behind you, please, Mr. Dawson," she said. "It's getting hot out there."

"You're going to need to do something about water and sanitation for all of these people," I said.

"Care for a root beer?"

She went to the refrigerator and popped the cap off a bottle without waiting for an answer, and handed it to me.

"I have a water well," she said. "And some of the kids that the army trained to kill people dug a slit trench in the field across the way."

"I did not just hear you say that," I said. "But between you and me, that is not your property to designate as a latrine."

She crossed the room, returned to her place on the sofa, and crossed her legs. "The truth is, I don't know if I can get these folks to leave even if I wanted to."

"You can see what's happening here. It's already getting out of hand. If those kids trespass on federal land, it'll bring the authorities down on you with both boots."

She hunched her shoulders and cast her eyes out the window.

"They brought this down upon themselves," she said. "I'm only shedding light on the issue."

"Being the first to speak out about something does not automatically grant you the moral high ground."

She turned her eyes on me, and her cheeks darkened with anger.

"I forgot for a moment that you're one of them." She placed special emphasis on the last word. "You lease grazing land from the BLM. You stand to benefit from the things that they do."

"That does not make me complicit in their actions, Ms. Pineu. Nor does it imply that I agree with their treatment of native horses."

"Let them arrest me."

I took a swallow from the bottle and set it on the counter. Dust motes swirled in agitated currents where the air vent vibrated near the windowsill.

"You're an honorable woman, Ms. Pineu, but if you don't put an end to this, it could blow up in your face and undermine your entire cause. The residents of this county won't be tolerant forever. They're sympathetic to you now, but that could turn with the occurrence of one ugly incident, and your credibility will go up in smoke. I don't want to see that happen."

She studied my face, then cast her eyes to the floor.

"You know I'm not wrong," she said.

I tried to shift the subject.

"I didn't see the Charlatans out there," I said.

"Those guys come and go. Maybe they left for good. Who knows?"

I wanted to believe that at least some small sliver of good fortune had shone down, but I did not hold much stock in a dependence on luck. I kept that small hope to myself.

"Please think about what I've told you," I said. "Before this reaches critical mass."

I closed the door softly behind me and stepped out into the afternoon sun.

CHAPTER SEVEN

CALEB WHEELER WAVED me over to the sorting pen as soon as I stepped out of the truck. He was horseback and I couldn't help but notice the well-worn stock of a lever-action carbine tucked inside a leather saddle scabbard that hung beside his leg.

"Problem?" I asked.

"Could be," he said. His eyes moved past me and squinted into the sun. "Looks like Dub Naylor's gone missing. Your dog showed up alone about half an hour ago. He was drifting about a dozen heifers in all by himself."

Jordan Powell and Samuel Griffin knelt in the loose dirt on the other side of the rail fence, turning their faces away from the ball of dust kicked up by the calf they had just branded and released. He bawled and kicked the air before he found his footing and ran through the chute into the paddock with the others.

"I'd wager Naylor's afoot," Powell shouted. "'Cause his horse committed suicide."

"I'll go," I said to Wheeler. "I could use some fresh air anyway."

Griffin dusted off his chaps, hopped the top rail and wandered in our direction.

"If it's all the same to you, Mr. Wheeler," Griffin said. "I'll go along with Mr. Dawson just in case he needs a hand."

Caleb looked from Griffin's face to mine. Whatever he was thinking, he was keeping it to himself.

"It might be wise to have another man along if you can spare him," I told Wheeler.

He glanced at his wristwatch and craned his neck to have a look at whatever progress was being made by the rest of the crew.

"I can set with that," he said and stepped out of the saddle. "You better sparkle up quick, though. You only got another three or four hours of daylight."

———

THE FIRST hour went by in a silence defined at first by small talk punctuated by long, companionable silences. I spoke of the ranch's long history, and Griffin told me about his football career and his pursuit of a college degree in husbandry.

"I heard one of the men call you 'Captain,'" he said as we topped a rise that looked out over the rolling hills to the north.

"Only Powell calls me that," I said. "Don't you start doing it."

He nodded and took off the sunglasses he had been wearing and slipped them into the breast pocket of the denim jacket he wore.

"You mind if I ask why he does that?"

I scanned his face for a moment and recognized no motive or artifice, so I answered him.

"Force of habit," I said. "I was in the army once. So was Powell."

thickets of timber and undergrowths of live oak runners, finding no sign of a struggle or anything else in the dry grass that had grown tall enough to brush the bottoms of our stirrups. We worked our way back to my side of the fence, careful to avoid snags on the tangle of fallen wire and wood. The surface of the pond was still in the failing light, strung with bunchgrass along the edges and clotted with blooms of algae and moss. Swirling gray clouds of lacewings and gnats, and the sweet green odor of stagnating water floated in the air as we lifted Dub's body and placed it gently across the saddle of his horse. I unfurled my rain slicker and covered him with it, and secured him with his own reata.

It was a different kind of silence that accompanied us down the hill, mournful and angry and not at all unlike the sensation I had long associated with the loss of a companion in battle. But this was murder, without purpose or explanation, and I carried the weight of Dub Naylor's death where it rested: squarely on my shoulders.

We picked our way down the trail in full dark. Insects buzzed in the tree line and would go suddenly still as we passed.

"This isn't on you, Mr. Dawson," Griffin offered.

His voice had the muted quality of a man speaking more to himself than another. It seemed we hadn't uttered a single word in quite some time.

"The hell it isn't," I said.

We topped the last hill of open pasture, and I climbed down to unhook the gate. I held it in place as Griffin rode past me, trailing the blue roan that carried Dub. He pulled up to a stop and waited for me while I looped the gate chain back into place.

I expected Griffin to move on ahead once I had remounted but he turned in his saddle instead.

"Do you mind if I ask you a question?" he asked.

"Go ahead."

"What is it like to own all of this?"

His question was one I had not been expecting. The ranch was one of the largest in this part of the state, in terms of deeded acreage, but I never truly thought of it as my own. It is not characterized by extravagant structures; the house Jesse and I lived in had not changed much in three generations. The barns and outbuildings had been constructed for service, not luxury, and it was the ranch and the cattle that always came first. I had been taught early and often that you sacrificed whatever you had to for the land, because God wasn't making any more of it. You never used debt, so you owned what you owned, and legacy was something your great-great-grandchildren might talk about.

I looked into the night sky and found the thumbnail scratch of a waning crescent hovering low on the horizon, and shook my head.

"I truly have no idea," I said.

He nodded, and I believe he understood what I meant.

CHAPTER EIGHT

MY HEADLIGHTS CUT a swath along the white line of the two-lane that was still deserted at this early hour of the morning. The hum of the highway and the whistle of wind blowing through my open window had grown monotonous, and I crushed my cigarette into the ashtray. I knew the only radio station I'd be able to receive between the steep walls of the canyon was an all-news channel, but I switched it on anyway.

> ". . . day twenty-six of the standoff at Wounded
> Knee has brought the arrest of so-called mercy pilot Bill
> Zimmerman on charges of conspiracy. In other news,
> Washington sources have reported that White House
> Counsel John Dean has told prosecutors that the break-in
> at the offices of Daniel Ellsberg had, in fact, been
> ordered by the White House itself, and the repercussions
> could result in the resignations of senior White House
> staffers H.R. Haldeman, the president's chief of staff, and
> domestic affairs advisor John Ehrlichman.
>   "Washington officials also announced today that
> government attorneys have requested that all bomb-related

charges associated with members of the radical group,
the Weather Underground, be dropped due to allegations
that tactics used by the FBI have been deemed illegal—"

I switched it off again. The radio had been a mistake.

"Jesus Christ," I said to no one, and watched the last curl of smoke slide out the window.

The acid in my stomach burned like a welding torch, and my head felt as if it were being methodically constricted inside of a band of razor wire.

I MADE a right onto a paved rural road whose only identifying marker was a mailbox that had been welded to a steel pillar with a name stenciled on it with reflective paint.

I drove only a short distance before I passed beneath a broad archway scrolled with decorative iron and climbing vines, beyond which the edges of the road had been planted with Italian cypress and decorative shrubs and terminated in a circular driveway that surrounded a stone fountain.

I pulled to a stop, got out, and walked up the short staircase to the front door. I rang the bell several times then went back to my truck. I leaned against the truck bed and lit another cigarette. Stray water drops fell from the bowls of the dormant fountain and made a sound like that of a kitchen faucet in need of repair.

The light fixtures that flanked the twin doors of the entry switched on and their brightness cut into my eyes as I stood waiting in the dark.

"What in the hell are you doing at my home at this hour?" Sheriff Lloyd Skadden said as he stepped outside. He raised a hand to his brow as a shield against the glare of the house lights and squinted in my direction. He was dressed in plaid flannel pajamas and a heavy wool bathrobe that hung to his ankles, his feet clad in leather-soled slippers.

"Step down here," I said. "I need you to see this."

I lowered the tailgate and pulled the canvas cover away from the wood box that rested in the bed. He peered over the side and I watched his expression change.

"You get that off my property," he said.

"You told me that the medical examiner would come pick him up last night. Nobody showed."

"You moved the body?"

"Of course I moved his body. If I hadn't he'd still be lying on the ground out there, wouldn't he?"

"Please put the tarp back down."

I ignored him and let him stare into Dub Naylor's face.

"I waited until one thirty this morning. I had to put him in a shipping crate filled with ice," I said. "Does that sound right to you?"

"I told you I'd get to the bottom of it. If the ME didn't show, that's on him."

"Like hell," I said. I flicked the remains of my burning cigarette in his direction. It exploded at his feet in a shower of sparks. "You'll call that sonofabitch yourself, right now, and have him come pick up my man."

Skadden balled his hands and shoved them into the deep pockets of his robe. His eyes darted between me and the box in my truck.

"You need to calm down, Dawson. I can't have an ME's report saying they retrieved a dead man from the driveway of my personal residence."

I took a step toward him.

"This man was murdered. On *my* land. Shot through the throat with a high-caliber weapon."

"You're not the sheriff, for God's sake, Dawson."

"You sure got me acting like one." I recalled my father's admonition never to trust a man who was unwilling to saddle his own horse.

His gaze cut away from me, in the direction of his tree-lined entry, and he seemed to lose three inches in height. I had not been to this place in years, not since before I had left for Korea. For all the fountains and landscaping, it held the appearance of the dwelling of a man in exile from his own homeland. His family's holdings had shrunk down to their last twenty acres, and Lloyd Skadden had fastened himself onto it like a life ring.

"You're nothing but a goddamned politician," I said.

"That's exactly the kind of politician I am," he said, and turned his face to me. "Don't make me regret giving a badge to you."

"I already regret it. But now that it's come this far I reckon you'll have to drill a pistol barrel up my nose and pry it out of my hand."

"Are you making some sort of threat?"

"People don't always agree with me," I told him. "But they rarely misunderstand what I say."

He combed a hand through his hair and tried to recover control of the situation.

"I said I'd look into what happened to your man there," he said and pointed a finger at me. "In the meantime I want that Pineu woman shut down like I told you before."

I shook my head.

"That train already left the station," I said.

"Then you'd better call it the hell back. I will not have federal agents taking over my jurisdiction."

He walked back into his house, but left the door open. Lights from inside glowed briefly and went dark again, then he came back onto the landing.

"You take these," he said and tossed me a key ring strung through with a heavy set of keys. "I forgot to give them to you before."

I held his stare as I hefted their weight in my palm.

"Don't look so confused," he said. "Those are keys to the lockup in Meridian. There's five or six holding cells in there. The next time you call me, it'd better be because they got too crowded."

—∽∿∾—

IT WAS nearly noon that same day by the time I returned to the ranch from the hospital where the medical examiner kept his office. My truck bed was empty and I had left the canvas tarp neatly folded on the seat, like the ceremonial flag from a military interment. I decided to leave it there as a reminder that in spite of appearances, some malevolent agent of transformation had begun to reveal itself, as though the people of this valley were being systematically poisoned. As a means to lift myself out of denial, anger would be as effective a tool for me as any.

Pale pink flowers blossomed on the dogwoods in the yard and wisteria climbed the trellis beside the gallery. A spider's web was strung between the uprights of the porch rail, and sunlight sparkled on the near-perfect circle still limned with dew. The creature that had constructed it was nowhere in sight.

The house was empty as I went into the mudroom, stripped off my clothes, and threw everything into the washer. The sleeves of my coat, my shirt, and the cuffs of my jeans were crusted with patches of dried blood. I took a long, scalding shower, dressed myself, and took a pan of hot water onto the porch to scrub my boots with a rag and brush to remove the blood that had seeped onto the welt.

The phone in the kitchen rang and I placed my boots in the sunshine to dry while I went inside to pick it up.

"There's two kids here in the office to see you," Caleb said.

"What kids?"

"Hell, I don't know. Hippie kids. I figured they're new friends of yours from the circus at Teresa Pineu's."

"I'll be right there."

"You know," he said. "I hope our little cattle business isn't interfering too much with . . . whatever this is turning into."

I hung up, pulled on my boots, and threaded my way down the long path to the office. A piss-yellow Ford Econoline van sat in the shade of a tree near the front door to the office. The back doors of the van were flung open, revealing a clutter of black cables and steel suitcases and a shoulder-mounted rig for a film camera. An Indian blanket had been strung from a cord that separated the cargo area from the driver, the interior walls ornamented with dozens of stickers. A familiar young man wearing aviator sunglasses sat on the bumper strumming an unplugged electric guitar that made the dull sound of a stick being scraped on a chain-link fence. He wore a Fu-Manchu mustache that grew down to his chin and he nodded blithely as I passed him and stepped into the office.

Caleb Wheeler looked up and grinned when I came in. He had been seated at his desk poring over an order form from a supply catalog while Samuel Griffin leaned against the wall, propped on one foot, and fashioning a hackamore from a length of rope. He was enjoying this too.

If the kid sitting in the corner on a hard wooden chair—in the sole and silent company of a grizzled cowboy three times his age and a broad-shouldered black man with his hat pulled down to his eyebrows—was the least bit uncomfortable, he didn't show it. In fact, he appeared rather pleased with himself.

"My name's Peter Davis," the kid said, then stood and offered his hand. "We met at Teresa Pineu's place down in—"

He wore an open-collared shirt embroidered with Mexican stitching, crushed corduroy bell-bottomed jeans, and a simple silver chain ornamented with a tooth from some kind of animal circling his neck.

"I remember you," I said and shook his hand. His hands were as soft as a woman's. "You're making a movie."

"A documentary," he corrected. "We're covering the whole thing about wild horses, the BLM, the government stifling free speech and assembly—"

I raised my hands in mock surrender.

"Save it," I said. "What are you doing on my ranch?"

"Last time I saw you, you told me to talk to the sheriff, and I did. I met with him this morning. He said if things were getting out of control at Teresa Pineu's, then I needed to see you about it. He said that you were the undersheriff in this part of the county, and that whatever went on down here was your responsibility."

His face seemed lit from within as he spoke, eyes misted, and carried himself with the inflated posture of a True Believer. It was the expression I associated with ideological fanatics driven by politics or religion that I'd been seeing so much of lately.

"You have the sheriff's statement on film?" I asked.

He nodded.

"The sheriff also told me that you lost a man yesterday."

I felt my face flush with heat, a taste in my mouth like burned copper.

"We didn't *lose* a man. Someone shot him in the throat and nearly took his head off his neck with a high-powered rifle. They dumped his body in a pasture and left him to be picked apart by coyotes. Did he mention that to you?"

"No, sir," he said. A little of the light had gone out of his eyes.

"This movie you're—"

"Documentary."

"Whatever," I said. "This documentary you're making, you intend to tell the truth? To *show* the truth?"

"Sure, man, of course."

I looked at Caleb, who had stopped grinning, then turned my eyes on Peter Davis.

"If you want the truth, you need to speak to the people who live here. You need to walk the streets of Meridian and see what is happening here, what all of this fuss is doing to them. This town is our lives. This place is my life. We all have the right to say what we want, but someone murdered one of my hands for no reason at all, and that kind of shit will not stand. Am I making myself clear?"

"Perfectly."

"I'll tell you what," I said. "You want some film? You want to see some reality, you come with me now. You know how to ride a horse?"

"We can't drive where we're going?"

"Not a chance. Answer my question."

"I've ridden a little."

"And your friend out there? He's your cameraman, right?"

"Yeah."

"Can he ride?"

"I guess so."

I nodded at Caleb, and he and Griffin were out the door to fetch three horses. While we waited, the two young men sifted through the back of the van for the equipment they'd need. A few minutes later, we mounted up. I eased my horse forward and addressed them from over my shoulder.

"There's not that much to it," I said. "Just keep your ass in the saddle and the pointy end headed in the same direction as me."

———⟨⟩———

TWO HOURS later, we crested the last rise that opened onto the North Camp pasture. The boys had handled themselves reasonably well on horseback once the animals settled in, and had shot film for what they called "b-roll" in various spots along the trail. They were doing more of it now, a slow pan across the wide expanse of forage and a zoom toward the pond and the spot where I'd discovered the body of Dub Naylor.

I twisted in my saddle and saw ribbons of smoke rising from the slash piles that burned in the bottomlands, and the stacks of felled timber awaiting the torch. A trio of carrion birds described slow circles against the sky and a breeze coming out of the south carried the smell of bruised grass and loam.

Peter signaled me that they had finished their wide shots, and I moved off toward the pond where we dismounted and I hobbled our horses.

"I want this on film," I said. I squatted on my haunches and indicated the patch of silage where Dub's body had been dumped. "We found him here. The bullet entered just below his Adam's apple and exited at the base of his skull. The hole in the front was smaller than a dime; in back it was the size of a golf ball. Why his head stayed on his shoulders is a mystery to me."

Peter blanched, but I continued, "There was little blood near the body, so we know he had been moved, but out here there is no way to know which direction the bullet had come from."

I stood and waited as the lens swept over the scene and I began to walk in the direction of the section of fence that had been pushed over. I was surprised to discover that it had been repaired, but tried not to show it to the camera.

"This section of fence had rotted out and been opened up by the herd. Cattle will often brush against the wire and posts, and if they break, the animals just keep on going."

Three sections of twisted barb had been replaced, together with the four-by-four upright supports. This would not have been easy work and would have required hours of digging and stringing, work which I had not ordered done by my crew.

"Stop the camera," I said.

It had been nearly dark by the time Griffin and I had found Dub's body, so we had not had the ability to conduct a proper search on the other side of the line. I intended to do it now. I gathered the horses and led them by the reins, returning to the spot where the movie boys waited. I reached into my saddlebag and retrieved a pair of wire cutters.

"Hey, man, are you supposed to do that?" Peter Davis asked.

"Old cowboy tradition," I said, laying the cutters across my palm. "This device is known as a 'Range Key,' and technically, no. But if you want to see the scene the way that it was when I found my man's body, this is how it gets done."

I led us in single-file through the narrow gap I had created and entered onto the untended rangeland that belonged to the government. The forage was tall enough to brush against our feet, and undulated in smooth waves where the wind channeled through.

I found the first sign of cattle flop on the opposite side of a thick copse of cedar. The grass had been trampled flat, and gave the appearance of having been grazed by a dozen animals or more.

"You can see here that my herd must have pushed through the old fence and drifted their way in this direction. Dub

Naylor would have come this same way to round up the strays so he could haze them back through the hole in the wire. You following me?"

The camera was running again.

We continued in a wide arc through rough terrain strewn with moss-crusted boulders the size of a car, and dotted with the burrows of voles and gophers. I counted at least six more spots where my cattle had settled during their trespass, and figured it must have taken hours for Dub to locate them all.

My eyes roamed the horizon, temporarily lost in thought, when my horse faunched and spooked, and threw his head wildly. It was then that I looked to the ground and saw that I had nearly run all three of us off the edge of a bluff that dropped nearly fifty feet straight down into a dry gulch.

Peter and his cameraman, whose name I couldn't remember, came to a halt and my heart pounded hard in my chest. I swung my leg over the cantle, dismounted, and stepped cautiously to the edge and looked over.

The neck of the swale was relatively narrow where I stood, maybe fifty yards across and cloaked in deep shadow by the steep angle of the afternoon sun. It opened gradually, like a Chinese fan, and spread to a width of at least a quarter of a mile, the bottom gray and smooth with crushed stone.

"I gotta get a shot of this, man," Peter said.

I helped them both down from their saddles and stood beside them on the rim of the gorge as they captured the sweep of the view.

"What the hell is that?" Peter asked. He was pointing some distance up into the throat of the chasm.

I shaded my eyes and squinted into the dark and finally saw it.

"It's fucking huge," the cameraman said. It was the first time I had heard him utter a word. "What is it?"

"Looks like a building," I said.

"No shit."

"I wanna get down there and check it out," Peter said.

"Not a chance," I told him, and glanced at my watch. "I'm not taking the horses down there. Too steep. It'll take hours to get to level ground, and hours to get back. We don't have that kind of time before the sun goes down."

"C'mon, dude."

"Besides, this is federal land."

The cameraman twisted his face into an expression that put me in mind of a spoiled child.

"What's your name again, anyway?" I asked.

"Sly."

"Sylvester," Peter corrected.

"Fuck you, man," Sly said, and returned his attention to the shadow below. "Seriously."

I led my horse away from the ledge and hoisted myself into the saddle.

"Let's go," I said. "We've seen enough."

In order to save time, I took a more direct northwesterly route back to the place where we had breached the fence. The sun was dipping lower along the crenellated outline of the mountains and bathing us in its glare. I pulled my hat down low on my brow in an attempt to keep my eyes in shadow and heard an odd brittle snapping sound beneath my horse's hooves. I pulled to a stop, looked down, and saw the skeletal remains of a heifer, the shards of its bones scattered over a broad patch of soil that looked as if the vegetation had been burned away by fire. It was exactly the same mutilation that Jordan Powell and I had come across only a few days before, only this one was much older.

"Hold up," I called out to Peter and Sly. "Get a shot of this."

They drew up on either side of me and turned their backs to the sun for a better view.

"What are we looking at? Are those bones?"

"It used to be one of my cows."

Sly hefted the camera to his shoulder and circled the blackened area on foot. When he was finished shooting, he tucked the heavy camera under his arm and looked into my face.

"It looks like it fucking *blew up*, dude."

"It does," I said. "And I've seen others just like it."

"Where?" Peter asked.

"Different places, mostly along this fence line."

"What is it?"

"Rustlers?" I said. "I don't really know."

"*Rustlers?* Is that still a thing?"

I pushed the brim of my Stetson back so that he could see my eyes when I answered him.

"I told you before: If you intend to tell the truth about what is going on in this valley, you better get off your ass and talk to the people who make their living on this land. Yes, rustlers are still a thing. Roundups are still a thing. They don't grow hamburger patties on a farm somewhere in Iowa. Teresa Pineu's stand against the treatment of wild horses is a thing. It's all a *thing*, goddammit."

Peter started to apologize, but I had had enough.

"A bunch of kids in tie-dye showing up with picket signs and incense doesn't mean a hill of shit if you don't get a handle on the whole story. Whatever good you might do here, or whatever trouble you bring down? It all remains right here long after you've all gone back to wherever the hell you came from. Before you poke the beehive, you'd better know what's going to come of it, and who's going to have to foot the bill for the fallout."

I pulled my hat back into place and turned my horse toward the sun.

"I don't know what you're standing there for," I said. "You'd better fork that saddle. We got a long damn way to ride."

CHAPTER NINE

JESSE WAS WAITING inside the barn when we returned that evening. She had prepared a tray of sandwiches and a pitcher of iced tea and was seated in a high-backed chair in the alcove where the saddles and tack were stored.

The final remnants of a lavender sky set the silhouettes of conifers into sharp contrast against it and the first glimpses of Venus and Saturn and Vega floated in the dim glow of the rising sliver of moon. Winged insects circled the lights outside the barn and cast a fluttering pattern of shadows on the hard ground.

We walked the horses inside and I tied each one in turn to hitch rails affixed to their stalls. Peter and Sly slid down from their mounts, stretched the kinks out of sore backs and legs, and moved off toward Jesse and the tray of food.

"Where are you going?" I said. "Horses eat first."

"Say what?"

"Those animals just carried 200 pounds of rider and gear over fifteen miles, and all you did was sit on your asses. We take care of them first."

Jesse filled glasses from the pitcher and brought them to us while we curried and combed sweat and trail dust from horsehide. The air was thick with the singular equine odors of sawdust and feed pellets, and the wet smacking sounds of grinding teeth; nostrils flared wide as they worked their jaws in anticipation.

The boys made a beeline for the food while I turned the animals loose in their stalls. I could hear the unintelligible mutter of voices when Jesse introduced herself and passed plates.

I unbuckled my chaps and hung them on a peg in the tack room, brushed myself off, and returned to kiss my wife's upturned cheek. Smile lines radiated from the corners of her eyes, bright with the light that they held when she was happy.

"I have a surprise for you," Jesse said.

She gestured toward the open door of the barn, and I watched as my daughter stepped in from the dark. She crossed the space in three steps and into my outstretched arms, and pressed her face into my chest. Her hair smelled of strawberries and sage.

"Hi, Daddy," she said.

"Welcome home, Cricket."

I held her at arm's length and looked into the clear blue eyes she had inherited from her mother, then drew her back in for another embrace. It had been barely three months since I'd seen her at Christmas, but I would have had a difficult time recognizing her in a crowd. She was dressed in a pair of form-fitted Bongo jeans, a white peasant blouse, and bare feet encircled by the narrow leather straps of Mexican sandals. Earrings fashioned from silver wire and pill-shaped beads of turquoise and coral dangled halfway to her shoulders.

"You've changed your hair," I said.

She fluffed it with her fingers, shook her head in the manner of a fashion model, and smiled.

"They call it a shag," she said. "You like it?"

I waited a beat too long, and it showed in her fallen expression.

"I like it," I said.

"No, you don't."

Jesse took our daughter's hand in hers and led her into the alcove where the two boys stood mutely, making no attempt whatsoever to disguise their interest.

"Put your tongues back in your mouths," I said. "This is my daughter, for God's sake."

Jesse shot me a look and introduced Cricket.

"This is Peter," she said. "And this is Sly."

They nodded a greeting, but made no attempt to shake hands or otherwise touch her, which I considered to be a good thing.

"They're making a film about the demonstration at Teresa Pineu's."

"A documentary," Peter said. This was an important distinction to him for reasons I had yet to comprehend. "They're protesting the slaughter of mustangs on BLM land. It's terrible, and the government is doing nothing about it."

"What do you expect?" I put in. "It's a *government program*."

They all frowned at me, and my daughter's cheeks flushed in either embarrassment or anger, or both.

"That's even worse," Cricket said. "It's Wounded Knee all over again."

"Yeah, exactly," Peter agreed.

"You'd better pray it isn't," I said. "They're trading gunfire with federal agents every night. People have been killed over there."

Peter puffed up with the look of righteous indignation I had seen earlier that day and his eyes went all misty again.

"If that's what it takes," he said.

I felt my own skin prickle with heat.

"Those are the words of a person who has never heard a shot fired in anger. There are other ways to get what you want."

"I just came from there," Cricket said.

"Came from where?" I asked.

"Pine Ridge. Wounded Knee."

"What the hell—"

Jesse's eyes met mine, and she appeared to be as shocked as I was.

"A bunch of us went there to support AIM," Cricket persisted. "They're being victimized."

"Far out," Sly said.

"Shut up, Sly," I interrupted, and he took a step back, like my words had assaulted his person.

"They're defending their rights!" Cricket's cheeks flushed pink. "Our own government's been lying and stealing from them for years!"

"That may be," I said. "But 200 militant Indians are going to die, and get nothing in the bargain."

"And that's okay with you?"

"Of course it's not," I said. "But I don't want my daughter to die with them."

At the back of the barn a horse nickered, and I heard the agitated pawing of hooves on the floorboards. I drew a deep breath and moved toward the cool air blowing in from the night.

"I'm sorry," I sighed. "I respect your passion. What I don't understand is how you can protest a war in Southeast Asia, but condone the provocation of one right here at home. People will die. Good people."

"We didn't start it."

"I know," I said and turned to face Peter Davis. "I've told you once already: You have the power to shape your story any way you choose, it's right there in your hands. Just be sure it's the truth. I've seen killing firsthand, and I can promise you that you don't want to see it yourself. Go ahead and fight your fight. It's a respectable one. But I warn you to be mindful about it; you may not recognize the wreckage after it's blown itself out."

The silence that followed was more than mere absence of sound, and the weight of it was both tangible and heartbreaking.

"I'm sorry," I said.

The fact was, I was tired of hearing moral and political lectures from children, so I excused myself and went up to the house for a smoke.

I was still standing on the gallery when Jesse came from the barn to join me a few minutes later.

"It isn't her fight," was all I could think of to say.

"Look who's talking."

Sometimes when the wind blew just right, I could hear snippets of sound from the bunkhouse where the hired hands slept: a few bars of a song, or shared laughter at someone's expense. Those sounds bore no distinction from those made by the cowboys and fence-riders employed by my forebears, and I felt insulated by the passage of time. The focus and function of the ranch and the care of its livestock took precedence here, in a form little different from the activities on ranches that predated the Civil War. We were isolated and safe, removed from the mechanized tick of the clock.

From below, near the office, I heard the muted patter of conversation among Cricket and Peter and Sly. Not many years ago it was rope swings, Shetland ponies, and pet squirrels. It seemed outside the natural order of things that nineteen years of accumulated joy could disappear in the span of a few short months.

"I swear to Christ," I said. My eyes burned in their sockets and I was grateful for the dark. "I don't know what I'm supposed to do in order to be a good father to that girl anymore."

———⌇⌇———

THAT NIGHT I was visited by dreams of incoming rounds and Chinese soldiers in quilted jackets breaching the wire and of feathers falling out of the sky. They had not been cast off by the wings of the Seraphim, but a swirling black murder of crows. I dreamt of a circle of fire, a pit lined in rocks, and of Indians whose fingers had been dipped in ochre, painting their faces in accord with ancient ritual, preparing for battle. Preparing to die.

CHAPTER TEN

I SKIMMED THE bodies of dead insects and leaves from the trough in the horse pen enclosure, and ran a cool stream of fresh water inside it. A cloud of starlings passed overhead several times and finally lighted on the loose, hoof-pocked soil. They pecked at the ground for only a few moments and took flight again.

Drambuie separated himself from the herd and walked slowly in my direction, poked his head between the fence rails, and nuzzled me with an expectant look in his eyes. He was still young, not much more than a colt, and was frequently playful with me in the mornings before settling in for real work. I reached into my pocket, snapped off the end of a carrot, and palmed it into his mouth.

Cricket came up beside me, leaned her elbows on the crossbeam, and watched the horse eat from my hand.

"You want to feed him?"

"Sure," she said, and I handed her the remains of the carrot. "Can I ride him today?"

"I think he'd like that."

"I've missed him."

"I'm sure he's missed you too."

She patted his neck and he pushed at her until she capitulated and scratched him between his ears the way she always did.

"You drink coffee?" I asked.

"Sometimes."

"I was going to go up and get some. Want to come with me?"

She looked away from Drambuie and into my face, and in those few seconds she seemed like my daughter again.

"In a little while maybe," she said. "I was going to take a walk."

"Stop by the office and say hi to Caleb. I know he'd be happy to see you."

Jesse was at the sink doing dishes when I came inside, the sleeves of her plaid flannel shirt rolled up past her elbows. Her hair was tied back with an elastic band and she turned when she heard me come in.

"We just finished breakfast," she said as I kissed her on the neck. "Want something?"

"I'll pour myself some coffee."

"Did Cricket find you?"

"Was she looking for me?"

From the corner of my eye, I saw Jesse studying me.

"I really don't know," she said, and returned her attention to the dishes.

——◦◦◦——

I USED the phone in the kitchen to call Sheriff Skadden at his office.

"He's not in," she told me.

The receptionist's reply was curt and her tone transmitted the pinched expression she'd worn when I met her, like she was sucking all of life's bitterness up through a soda straw. I let go of any residual guilt I may have carried for my earlier unkind assessment of her personality.

"When will he be back?"

"No idea."

"Can you give him a message for me?"

I could hear the rattle of a flagpole chain and the popping of windblown canvas spinning down at me from her end of the line.

She sighed audibly. "Go ahead."

"Please thank him for sending the young filmmakers to see me. We had an enlightening conversation."

"Is that it?"

"No," I said. "One more thing: Please pass along my gratitude for seeing to it that my busted fence got mended so quickly, though it may need a little more attention. Seems somebody might have snipped the wires again."

"Excuse me?"

"Have we got a faulty connection?" I asked.

"The connection is fine."

"The name is Dawson."

"I got it the first time."

"D-A-W-S-O-N."

Jesse was staring at me as I broke the connection and placed the receiver back on its hook.

"What is the matter with you?" she asked.

"I don't know what you're referring to."

"I've seen that look before, Ty, back when we worked in Hollywood. It's like the slide that precedes an ugly fall. I've never seen it on you."

"Just taking care of some things," I said. "There's getting to be too many piglets for the teats."

—◦◦◦—

CRICKET WAS running Drambuie around a barrel course she'd set up in the arena when I brought my coffee out to the gallery. I never tired of watching a good horse and rider at work, the mutual trust that they shared, and Boo had always had the lungs and legs to run the outside circle. She leaned forward and lay low along the pommel while he opened up his gait for the return run, and I lost her inside a cloud of dust when Boo hunched his hindquarters, dug in his hooves, and skidded to a stop. I heard the cowboys whistle and applaud.

Wyatt scurried up from the arena, took the stairs two at a time, and lay on the floorboards beside my boots, his pink tongue hanging out from his snout. I knelt and rubbed his head before I went back indoors to top off my mug.

I was pulling the plug on the percolator when Wyatt began to bark in the way that he does only when he's distressed, and it captured my immediate attention. When I returned to the porch, I saw what had him so agitated.

Eli Corcoran straddled a dapple-gray stock horse and had walked him straight up to the porch rail. Both horse and rider looked parched and hard-used.

Jesse came out from the back of the house where she had been hoeing fresh rows in the vegetable garden.

"What's got that dog so riled up?" she said, the last of her words trailing off as she also caught sight of the old man.

I shushed Wyatt and told him to sit on the stoop and I went to speak with our neighbor. I placed a hand on the horse's withers and looked up into Corcoran's lined face.

"I come by for a word with your grandpap," Eli said, crossing his arms over the horn of his saddle and leaning down toward me. "Can you fetch him for me, son?"

I glanced sidelong at Jesse and she read my expression.

"I'll go take a look inside," she told him. Her lips flattened into a narrow line and she moved hastily into the house to phone Snoose.

"You look a little thin at the equator," I said. "Why don't you climb off and let us scare up a bite for you."

He searched my face for a long moment and seemed to be translating my words. He patted a saddlebag that was strapped on behind him, and I noticed he'd tied on a bedroll as well. Wherever he thought he was going, he had planned for an overnight trip.

"Thanks just the same," he said. "But Miss Marie packed me a kit before I rode out this morning."

"Your horse could use some water, too, I expect," I persisted. I smiled and took gentle hold on the reins where they hung loose from the snaffle.

"You got a point there."

"I'll water your horse while you take a seat on the porch. Jesse'll bring you a glass of iced tea."

Eli Corcoran swung a bony leg over the saddle and dismounted. I could feel the slight tremor of his hand when he gripped my shoulder to thank me, his expression bemused and his eyes like blue milk. He looked past me and into a distance and seemed to recede for an instant, into a place where round bales rested in fresh-mowed green fields and barn roofs caved in on themselves from nothing more than the passage of time.

I kept my eyes tight to the ground.

A train whistle blew from some other part of the valley and he came back into himself.

"I'd prefer you don't tell my son about this, but I've been seeing spirits with some regularity lately. I don't like to think on it too hard," he said and ambled slowly toward the house.

I led the horse to the trough and watched Jesse carry a pitcher and tray of glasses out to Eli. I let the horse drink his fill and hitched him to a post in the shade of a red maple.

Jesse was seated on a wicker chair beside the old man and nodding her head as he spoke. He turned to me when he noticed I'd come back.

"You s'pose you could spare one of them store-bought smokes you carry?"

I shook one out of the pack and lit it for him.

"Like I was saying," he said, resuming whatever he'd been speaking about with Jesse. I took a seat on the glider. "We trailed some beeves down to Old Mexico and when we was done I wired Miss Marie and she and her sister and her sister's husband—can't remember his name—all came down and joined me there for a vacation trip. We had a fine time."

"Sounds beautiful," Jesse said.

"The sister was a water witch. Did I ever tell you that?"

"I don't think you ever did."

"We held hands and walked down this little back street that was paved with nothing but round stones that looked like baked bread rolls. Kinda hard to walk on with boots, I remember. It was hot and so quiet that day, but somebody was playing a piano. The music was coming out of a house somewhere on that street, and we followed the sound 'til we found it. Sure enough, it was coming down from a third-story window of a building that looked like it was made from nothing but plastered-over mud bricks, all painted white. The windows had iron bars over them. Even so, somebody inside there had a piano, and they was playing something so pretty and sweet."

As I listened to him it came to me again that this man had been born in an era of transition, perhaps the last generation to know a nation that was more agrestic than industrial, where the insulated wires and poles that stretched across miles of rangeland carried messages tapped out on a telegraph key. But the voices that now drew his attention were those that no one else heard, and whose disclosures belonged solely to him.

"We sure had a fine time," he said.

Snoose Corcoran pulled up in his five-window flatbed and got out with the engine still running. He acknowledged both Jesse and me with a nod of his head, but his eyes remained fixed on his father.

"Hello, son," Eli said. "Come on and join us."

"We'd better get home, I think."

Eli reached over and scratched Wyatt on the flat of his head, and his knuckles went white when he latched onto the arms of his chair and hoisted himself to his feet.

"Thank you for the hospitality," he said. "I enjoyed the visit."

"Anytime," Jesse said and gave him a gentle kiss on the cheek. "You know that."

Snoose tried to take hold of his father's elbow as he started down the porch stairs, but the old man shook him off.

"I may be old, but I can still walk by myself, damn it. And I can still throw a string better 'n you can."

I walked Snoose to his truck and we both waited as Eli folded himself into the passenger seat. Snoose leaned in close and whispered an apology.

"There's nothing to be sorry for, except maybe he's not twenty years younger," I said. "And don't worry about the horse. I'll get him back to you."

"I'm not kidding, Ty, the old man's starting to spook me. He was talking to Mama when I walked into the kitchen this morning."

I didn't know what to say, so I didn't say anything, honored Eli Corcoran's wishes and kept the man's earlier confidence to myself.

Jesse stepped up beside me and wrapped an arm around my waist. We waved as Snoose threw the truck into gear and began to pull away.

Eli leaned out the window, cupped a hand to the side of his mouth.

"You tell your grandpap I'm sorry I missed him," he hollered.

If there is a sadder sight than a once-vital man brought to fear and confusion, I have not seen it.

—◦◦◦—

SHADOWS HAD begun to fall across the paper targets I had tacked to the straw bales in the meadow a good half mile from the ranch. I did not want to spook either the horses or the help with the shooting I was doing in an effort to clear my head. I slid the last six cartridges of Sellier & Bellot .357 ammunition out of the box and into the cylinder, clicked it into place, took up my stance, and sighted down the barrel of the Colt.

I had been at it for nearly an hour, emptying no fewer than 150 rounds in the process, but I'd planted every one of my last thirty shots inside the eight-ring from twenty-five yards. The final six had been no exception.

I plucked the cotton from my ears and ejected the spent shells into my hand. They were still hot to the touch and the air smelled of sulfur and ammonia and left the roof of my mouth tasting like I had sucked on a fistful of pennies. It was an altogether satisfying sensation.

"Blowing off a little steam?" Caleb Wheeler asked as he came up behind me. "Been that kind of day?"

"It's been that kind of week."

He followed as I strode across the swale to retrieve the tattered remnants of my targets. A tangle of wild primrose and salmonberry had begun to bloom around the base of the hay bales.

"I spoke to the medical examiner on the phone this afternoon," I said.

"What'd he say?"

"Nothing I didn't already know," I said, studying the holes I'd made in the paper and wadding the spent paper targets into balls. "All he would tell me was that Dub had been shot from an upward angle. He said that Lloyd Skadden directed that any further information go through him and not me."

Caleb buried his hands inside the pockets of his jacket and gouged a hole in the soft soil with the pointed toe of his roughout boots.

"Has Dub got any family around here?" I asked. "Anybody we can call?"

"I'll look into it. Jordan Powell might know. Those two were pretty close."

"Goddammit," I said. "A young man gets shot out of the saddle for no reason at all. What the hell is that?"

Caleb looked off into the pines and said nothing for a long moment.

"Cricket came by the office this morning," he said in an attempt to lighten my mood. "She's growing into a fine young lady."

"She has her moments."

He attempted to camouflage a smile as he smoothed his mustache with his fingers.

"I heard."

"What's that supposed to mean?" I asked.

"The office ain't that far from the barn, Ty. Voices carry."

In the distance, I could see rain sheeting the sky at high altitude, but down here on the ground it was cool and dry and brittle with thorny sunlight.

"Seems to me you could use a break," he said. "Meet me at the Blossom later on?"

"What the hell," I said, and saw a flash of lightning inside that far-off bank of clouds.

CHAPTER ELEVEN

I PARKED THE Bronco in the lot beside the post office, got out, and glanced up the length of Meridian's main street. The red leaves of the plum trees that had been planted along the sidewalk shimmered in the fading light, alive with the roosting clatter of grackles and junco. The small shops, bank, and feedstore had already closed for business, but Leo's Liquor and the Rexall still had their doors propped open, and the blue rings of neon tubing that circled the apron of the Richfield station glowed like a beacon on the corner.

The ball of keys that Sheriff Skadden had given me weighed heavy in the pocket of my Carhartt, and I used the hour I had to kill by making a visit to the small substation the sheriff's office maintained in town. The place was a dark vacuum of stillness when I stepped inside, the air stale, heavy with moisture and the sickly sweet odor of wood beetles. A fine layer of dust dulled the surfaces of two misshapen desks in the main room and the wire-glass partition that screened the rank of metal file cabinets in the back was littered with postings and memoranda that were curled up at the edges and fastened with cellophane tape that had gone brittle and yellow with age. I flicked a wall switch and the overhead lights stuttered to life and reflected off dust motes suspended in the atmosphere with a dull violaceous light.

I crossed to the rear of the room and passed through a door at the base of a narrow stairway that led up to the holding cells. My boots echoed loudly on the linoleum treads as I climbed the stairs, swallowed by the dark. I touched the handle of the Colt revolver tucked into the holster at my waist, and immediately felt like a fool. I ran my hand along the wall to find another light switch and blinked my eyes against the unaccustomed brightness when they finally flickered on.

This room seemed every bit as doleful and disused as the one below, only somehow more malevolent for its purpose. A single desk and wooden chair were positioned at an angle facing inward, between two grime-encrusted windows where the walls met in the far corner. Three holding cells constructed from vertical iron bars and steel mesh occupied the remainder of the space, their doors left ajar on hinges whose bolts and strike plates were crusted with layers of cracked and peeling paint and the mummified silken nests of insects long since dead.

If Sheriff Skadden or his deputies had ever spent much time at this end of the valley, or Meridian in particular, they'd left little evidence of it here.

I hadn't checked the phone lines downstairs, so I lifted the receiver of the one up here, a heavy Bakelite rotary with a cable sleeved in woven cloth that had been gnawed on by rodents. To my surprise, there was a dial tone.

I shut off the lights behind me as I left, with a malignant combination of depression and anger at having been manipulated overtaking me by the time I stepped back onto the street and locked the door. I tugged at the sleeves of my coat and wondered if it was possible for a human soul to be sucked out through the pores of exposed skin.

The streetlights had come on while I had been inside, though it would be at least another hour before the sun had fully set. I slid the keys back into my pocket, walked slowly up the street and through a rectangle of light that spilled across the sidewalk from the glass doors of the Alpha Beta market, whose mere existence in that moment seemed to help revive the sensation of my own waning sentience.

—◦◊◦—

THE COTTONWOOD Blossom had been a fixture in Meridian since the very first ranches had been established. The date carved into the capstone above the door read 1891. Its name alluded to a slang term used by old-time cowboys, and referred to a recipient of frontier justice who had later been discovered dangling at the end of a knotted rope, most frequently a cattle thief.

The room was fairly large by the standards of Meriwether County, but the Friday crowd had only begun to wander in. It was still the dinner hour and the atmosphere inside remained relatively subdued.

The paneled walls were festooned with the expected jetsam and detritus of a cow-town roadhouse: ancient poster advertisements from rodeos and fairs, rusted highway signs riddled with holes shot from the windows of passing vehicles, and the mounted heads of horned animals. On the joists that supported the tin-stamped ceiling over the duckboards, someone had tacked several pairs of women's panties and a collection of brassieres.

I took a stool at a C-shaped bar that had been crafted from rough-hewn planks of black oak, propped a boot heel on the brass rail, and watched the last of the muted daylight disappear behind the frosted pane of glass embedded in the front door. Neon beer signs buzzed beside the liquor bottles lined up along the shelves, and the owner, Lankard Down-ing, was jawboning with a customer as he counted change from the antique cash register at the far end of the bar, so I watched the beer tap leak foam onto the drip pan while I waited. Downing looked as pinched and sour-faced as always, but he nodded in my direction when he finally saw me there, then promptly disappeared into the stockroom without coming over to take my order.

I drummed my fingers on the scarred bar top and scanned the room while a Wurlitzer jukebox spun 45 rpm records by Donna Fargo and George Jones. My attention landed on a trio of old-timers wearing snap-button shirts and pressed blue jeans passing a dice cup at a four-top pressed up against the wall. They were sipping bottled beer they chased with red whisky in a manner that suggested a weekly ritual.

When I finally turned my head away, I found Lankard Downing's vulpine face staring at me like he'd been waiting for some time.

"What can I do you for, Dawson?" he asked.

It was an expression I had always detested, but in his case described an accurate declaration of his intentions.

"Olympia."

"Draft or bottle?"

"Draft," I said, and turned toward the room again while he set off for the tap.

The young man he had been speaking with earlier sat alone at the opposite end of the bar, hunched over an Old Fashioned glass filled with cracked ice and amber liquid. He poked at the contents with a plastic swizzle stick and stared into it like he was memorizing scripture. His head was angled in such a way that I couldn't see his face, but his reddish hair was long and dangled past his chin. He was dressed in faded denim jeans and matching jacket whose sleeves had been razored off at the shoulders, and wore a beard that he kept trimmed close to the skin. He must have sensed the weight of my gaze resting on him, because when he lifted his head he looked directly into my eyes. I nodded briefly, in the way you do when you've been caught gawking, and casually swiveled my stool in the opposite direction.

Lankard Downing slid my pint across the counter and I took the glass and moved to a table near the back that gave me a view of the entire room. An open archway in the far wall opened onto a room that had long ago been annexed from a space that had once been a bakery, but now contained coin-operated billiard tables, a couple dart boards, and a pinball machine with a lightning bolt of fractured glass across the scoreboard.

Two men wearing faded and sun-damaged motorcycle leathers were shooting pool and drinking beer out of a pitcher, and bore a striking resemblance to the pair of goons who'd tried to brace me at Teresa Pineu's place. Their vests were stitched with patches ornamented with artwork that identified them as members of the Charlatans MC.

"You got a minute, Ty?"

I looked up and into the face of Chandle Meeghan. He was a man I'd known for years as the owner of the feed and hardware store in town, but only in passing, and from his periodic presence at the church Jesse and I attended. He was a fifty-some-odd-year-old widower with the lined and worried affect of a man who carried a great and perpetual burden.

"Sure," I said. "Take a seat."

"I'm sorry to bother you, but I think I've got a problem."

I shot a glance in the direction of the bar and saw Lankard Downing working a damp rag along the bar, keeping one eye on our conversation.

"I called Lloyd Skadden's office about this a couple days ago," he said. "But I never heard back from him. Then Lankard phoned me and said that you were here. He told me you're the undersheriff now, and figured you'd be the man to talk to. So I came right over."

I removed my hat, hung it on the backrest of an empty chair beside me and smoothed my hair with my fingers. I did it as a stall for time while I took a deep breath and calmed myself from a surge of annoyance that made me want to stride across the room and drop Lankard Downing to the floor.

"What's the problem?" I asked, and took a draught from my glass.

"Emily's gone missing again."

"How long has she been gone?"

"Three, four days, I guess." He kept his eyes locked on the tabletop and would not look at me directly.

Chandle Meeghan was locally famous for the thick mane of hair that had gone from brown to stark white in the space of just a few weeks. That had been about the time his only daughter, Emily, turned fifteen. She was twenty or so now, I supposed, and widely known to possess a free spirit, a lazy mind, and the absence of any semblance of a moral compass or personal character. She was a wild child who had been gifted with considerable beauty, but had logged a long and checkered pattern of extremely poor choices.

"No idea where she might have gone off to? Friends or relatives, maybe?" I asked.

"You know how she is," he shrugged and still could not manage to look me in the eyes, and I felt sorry for him all over again.

"Have you got a picture of her, Chandle? Something I can show to people when I ask around."

He slid a photo from a clear celluloid frame sewn into his wallet and passed it to me. I planned to show it to Teresa Pineu. It seemed a likely place to start, but I mentioned nothing about that to him.

"I have to be straight with you, Chandle," I said. "She's over eighteen. A legal adult. She's got the right to go wherever she pleases. I assume you understand that."

He nodded and finally looked at me. His eyes were watery, the whites shot through with tiny pink veins.

"I can't make her come back home," I said. "I just need to know she's all right."

He stood and started to walk away, then came back to shake my hand.

"Thank you, Ty," he said. "I mean it."

"I have a daughter too."

I leaned the chairback to the wall, balanced on two legs, and finished my beer in two long gulps as I watched Chandle Meeghan stop to whisper something to Downing, then push the door open to leave.

I looked at my watch and saw I still had fifteen minutes before Caleb Wheeler was due to join me, and questioned my own decision-making process at allowing him to persuade me to come here in the first place. I watched a man feed a handful of quarters into the jukebox while I lit a cigarette and signaled to Lankard Downing for another beer.

I was joined, without preamble, by the reddish-haired man from the bar. He dropped into the chair Chandle Meeghan had just vacated and pushed a fresh pint and a shot of tequila across the table at me.

"Looks like you could use this," he said.

He was younger and much larger than he had originally appeared from a distance, a man built for decisive action, but his eyes were lit up with something resembling amusement.

"I'll pass on the tequila," I said. "It has a tendency to lull me into a false sense of calm right before it rips the hinges off of doors I try to keep shut."

"It won't go to waste," he said and tossed back the shot himself.

"But thanks for the beer."

"You know, Mr. Dawson, I usually don't like to be stared at when I'm surreptitiously staring at others."

"I assume the bartender gave you my name."

"Your man Lankard is a fountain of local information."

"He's not my man."

"I wouldn't think so," he said and it was his turn to smile. "Name's Rex Blackwood."

He offered a firm grip and I noticed the tattoo on his forearm.

"Navy?"

"SEAL Teams," he said. "But that seems like a long time ago."

"Couldn't have been that long."

On the dance floor in the corner, a couple of overweight tourists swayed beneath an electric oscillating fan that had been screwed into the wall overhead and pushed silver clouds of cigarette smoke around the room. The woman had squeezed herself into a tight pair of jeans that wrapped her thighs like sausage skin, but they gazed at one another with expressions of inebriated joy, so kept my unkind judgments to myself.

"What is that song?" Blackwood asked.

"No idea."

"Whatever it is, those two should not be dancing to it," he said. "Like a pair of cows skidding on a patch of ice."

My eyes cut sideways, toward the billiard room. The two bikers had replenished their pitcher and taken up stools at a

high table. They were making no effort to disguise their interest in Blackwood and me.

"Friends of yours?" I asked.

"Because of the way I'm dressed?"

"It delivers that impression."

Blackwood studied his drink in the same way he had before.

"Those guys are bad news," he said finally. "There were
three of them earlier. I ran into them over at the Richfield station when I was topping off my tank. They were filling jerry
cans with gas. What would three bikers be doing with jerry
cans?"

I waited him out and took a pull at my beer.

"One of them accosted me with a firearm," Blackwood said.
"So I hosed him down with the pump I had in my hand."

"Why are you telling me this?"

"You seem like a man who appreciates facts," he said. "I'm
not affiliated with those assholes. I'd rather you didn't think of
me as a biker. I'm more of a motorcycle enthusiast."

"You have an oblique way of speaking with people."

"You live in an interesting town."

"We've got trouble enough," I told him. This conversation
had taken on unsettling overtones. "You plan on staying long?"

Blackwood shrugged.

"I could use a bed and shower for the night. Got any
suggestions?"

"There's a motel about twenty minutes south of here."

"Saw it," he said. "Not exactly my speed. It seems a
little . . . rustic. My interests lie farther north, anyway."

"It's a good two hours or more to Lewiston. But I'm sure
you'll find more agreeable choices up that way."

Blackwood's eyes shifted to a point somewhere over my
shoulder. I turned to see the two Charlatans swaggering toward
our table.

"Something I can help you with?" I said.

"We thought that was you," the rabbit with the mustache said. "I couldn't be sure, since last time I saw you the barrel of your pistol was drilled into my eyeball."

His companion's face split into a lopsided grin, and made him seem more bovine than before. He had the flat and oblivious aspect of a baking pan, and his eyes bulged out from their sockets like Fritz Lang's.

"Didn't he call you a greasy fuck last time we met?"

"I do believe he did."

"As amusing as your Mutt and Jeff routine is," I said. "I think you need to pack your Samsonites and head on down the road."

Blackwood stretched and broke into an exaggerated yawn.

"Are we boring you?" the one with the rabbit face asked.

"More than you could possibly know," Blackwood said, and his face took on a curious, detached expression, like a man watching a rat in a wire cage through the window of a pet shop. "I'd rather mow the lawn than listen to you two fucktards. By the way, how's your buddy doing? He seemed a little miffed with me the last time I saw him."

Rabbit crossed his arms and glared at Blackwood. His eyes seemed to vibrate inside their sockets, the pupils spun down to pinpricks, and his sweat gave off an electric, medicinal odor.

"Nice seeing you again, cowboy," he said to me, and made the shape of a pistol with his thumb and forefinger. He trained his focus on Blackwood. "And I'm sure we'll be seeing *you* later."

"Not unless I want you to, you won't," Blackwood smiled.

I took a draw off my cigarette and crushed the butt into the ashtray as I watched them push through the door without a backward glance. These were men for whom I had no frame of reference, men without apparent purpose or destination in their lives, unfamiliar with human experience apart from the sting of loose highway gravel on their skin, the hum of pharmaceuticals in their bloodstreams, and the mechanical vibration of raw horsepower in their loins.

"Five minutes with you guys, and all I want to do is scrub the inside of my skull with a wire brush," I said to Blackwood.

The front door flew open again without warning, and the first thing that I noticed was the weapon. The biker with the mustache stood alone, a momentary silhouette against the pink light of the streetlamps, with a sawed-off shotgun dangling from one hand at waist level. The stock had been planed and sanded to the size and shape of a pistol grip and the barrel chopped off just beyond the magazine and forend. What happened in the next few moments seemed to unfold in kaleidoscopic fashion.

The eruption from the barrel of the sawed-off looked like a channeled blast from a smelting furnace and blew the bar mirror and the shelves of bottled liquor into tiny diamonds of sparkling glass. A woman's scream from behind me was drowned out by the crash of chairs and upturned tables as patrons scrambled to find shelter.

I tipped our four-top on its side and drew my revolver. Blackwood hunkered down beside me with a semiautomatic pistol that had somehow appeared inside his fist. I peered over the table's edge in time to see the gunman swing the barrels in my direction. His next blast slammed into the tabletop, rocked us backward, and I heard the whistle of stray pellets crease the air beside my ear. He jacked the spent shell casing and it rolled across the floor, then loosed another round that ripped the stuffing from the booth three feet to my left.

The room was choked in a haze of smoke and bits of foam padding that shimmered in a fleeting wedge of light as the biker backed his way outside.

I thumbed the hammer and loosed a shot that went wide and bored into the doorframe. My second went low and I heard it whang off the floor with the sound like the broken string of a guitar, but the ricochet caught the shooter in the ankle and swept him off his feet halfway out onto the sidewalk. His partner dragged him out before I could squeeze off a third shot and the room went deathly still.

I made a move to follow the bikers, but Blackwood took hold of my elbow.

"That model holds five shells," he said. "He'll take your head clean off your shoulders if you step outside that door."

"See if anybody's been hurt," I said, and made for the back exit instead.

I circled the rear of the building and moved up a narrow alley that smelled of standing water and spoiled food, my Colt held tight in a two-fisted grip. I paused when I reached the corner where the alley let onto the sidewalk and heard the hammering roar of Harley engines accelerating up the street toward the state road and stepped out in the open. I sighted down the barrel as the two bikes passed beneath a streetlight and disappeared into the dark.

The night went unnaturally quiet. The birds inside the maples had all gone still and even the shouts and emergent chaos inside the Blossom were frangible and muted. Beside me, at the edge of the curb, a tin sign advertising Green Stamps swung soundlessly from rusted hooks inside a metal frame and I noticed my ears had begun to ring.

There were no wailing sirens, no noticeable response of any kind until a couple of volunteers jogged over from the firehouse down the block. If I had previously harbored any illusions regarding professional support of any kind from Lloyd Skadden, it was time to let them go. The rhythm of my own breath reverberated through the blunted wall of my impaired hearing and I felt a rage grow in my chest until it burst like a line of surgical stitches popping one by one.

I knelt outside the front door of the Blossom and examined the trail of blood drops that led to the lip of the gutter and disappeared. When I stood, Caleb Wheeler was jogging toward me from wherever he had parked. He followed me inside the Blossom and took in the damage.

"Looks like things got a little Western in here," was all he said.

———

IT WAS approaching midnight by the time I returned to the ranch.

My hearing had recovered in the hours since the shooting, and the music from the wind chime Cricket and Jesse had strung inside the branches of our willow resonated sweetly on the breeze as I stepped inside the house.

Jesse came out from our bedroom while I filled a glass with tap water in the kitchen. She was wrapped in a soft cotton bathrobe and wore a pair of fleece-lined moccasins, and squinted at me in the meager light that glowed from the fixture above the sink, marks from the pillow imprinted on her face.

"Everything okay?" she asked. "You look like you've been rode pretty hard."

"I'm fine, Jess," I said. "Go on back to bed. I'll be there in a couple minutes."

She eyed me, and even half-asleep she knew me to my core. "What's wrong?"

"Nothing," I lied. "I'm just going out to chain the gate. I'll be right back."

"Excuse me?"

I had no desire to have this discussion at this hour of the night, but it appeared that the horse was now out of the barn.

"And I want you to keep the house locked up from now on," I added. "Especially when I'm not here."

We hadn't locked the doors or closed the road gate in over twenty years.

"You'd better talk to me, Ty."

"It's a precaution is all. This undersheriff stuff is grating on my nerves."

She cocked her head and crossed her arms, and I knew I wasn't going to bed anytime soon.

"Is there any chance at all that we could have this conversation tomorrow?" I asked.

"Nope," she said and sat down on the sofa. "Not even a tiny one."

CHAPTER TWELVE

I WALKED DOWN the steps of the gallery and headed for the bunkhouse where I had asked Caleb to gather the hands. Dry gravel crushed beneath my boot soles and shafts of sunlight broke through pinholes in the cloud cover and speared the valley floor.

The wellspring of rage that had been tapped the night before did not diminish with the arrival of a new day. I had not held any prior animosity at having been pressed into service by Lloyd Skadden, despite the fact that it had not been of my choosing. But it had already cost the life of Dub Naylor, not mine, someone who had not been privy to my own decision process. I would not abide the construction of victims, so the game was about to change.

It was quiet inside when I pushed through the door, no sign of the usual roughhouse I associate with hired cowboys during Spring Works. Their bunks had all been straightened, tack and gear hung on hooks, and the atmosphere was one of sober gravity. The room was thick with equine odors and those of men living in close quarters, and the snap of orange flames in the woodstove the only sound.

Caleb Wheeler nodded a wordless greeting to me and they stood as one when I took my place at the front of the room, in a fashion reminiscent of my military service. When I suggested that they all could be seated, not a single man did so.

"This won't take long," I said.

I removed my hat, held it by the brim, and looked each man in the eye, one by one.

"We all mourn the death of Dub Naylor," I began. "And I regret that I don't know any more about the nature of his murder than I did when Samuel and I first found him. I can't tell you why someone shot him, but I can say with a fair degree of certainty that it had nothing to do with anything he did."

My mouth went dry and I felt the edges of my anger creep in on me again.

"The responsibility is mine. I owe him—and each of you—an apology for that. You've all heard by now that I've been appointed as acting undersheriff for the south end of this county. I did not ask for that job, nor do I want it. But I've got it anyway.

"Things have gone to hell in the past few days, and no matter what you think about wild mustangs, or the BLM, or the kids camped out in protest down at the Pireu place, this whole damned town is at risk of . . . I don't know what.

"I thought it would all blow over," I sighed out loud. "But I was obviously wrong about that."

The woodstove popped an ember out through the open door, and sounded like a rifle shot. It smoked and glowed on the floorboards for a moment before one of the hands crushed it out under his boot heel.

"I need two volunteers," I continued. "Two men who know how to use a firearm, and who know how dangerous this situation might become. I need somebody who can watch my back the way that I'll watch yours."

Jordan Powell began to raise a hand.

"Hang on," I said. "I need you all to hear me out. I know that most of you don't even live here, but I can tell you that from what I can see, it can spread to your town just as easily.

"A young woman has gone missing. One of our cowboys has been murdered. And someone tried to punch my ticket with a sawed-off shotgun while I sat at a table in the Cottonwood Blossom last night.

"You don't have to answer me now. In fact, I don't want you to. Think hard on it, and if it's something you think you'd be suited for, come see me tomorrow. That's all I've got."

I made a move to turn away, but remembered something else.

"One more thing," I said. "Tomorrow is Easter Sunday. Anybody who wants to join me and my family for services in town is welcome to come along with us."

———

I STOPPED off at the barn for a few quiet minutes with Drambuie. I could hear him shuffle and pace inside the confines of his stall when he heard me come in.

I unclipped the stall guard and he poked his big head over the top of the door, where it bobbed up and down like a dashboard toy. I chipped slices of apple with a bone-handled knife, and he nuzzled my chest when I stepped forward to feed him. He studied me with clear, shiny eyes that were the color of chatoyant quartz as he chewed.

I mucked out his stall and rolled in a wheelbarrow load of fresh sawdust, then raked it out evenly over the mat. I scratched his muzzle and allowed him to search my empty pockets one last time before I left, slipping the gate latch behind me.

I took the back way up to the house, past patches of wild crocus and daffodils that Jesse augmented with bulbs of iris that had only begun to display their first sprouts. I wondered at the absence of Wyatt, who usually accompanied me whenever I went down to the bunkhouse where the hands often spoiled him with food scraps and chunks of venison jerky. My question answered itself when I saw a familiar piss-yellow van parked in the driveway beside the rear door to the house.

Jesse showed me a smile that was mostly sincere, but laced through with duplicity and a subtle warning for me to be nice. Cricket was seated at the kitchen table with Peter Davis, the young filmmaker, smoothing butter and slices of cheese and bologna onto bread they'd laid out in assembly-line fashion.

"Hi, Dad," Cricket said without explanation and without looking up from her work.

"What's all this?" I asked.

"They're making food for the kids at Teresa's," Jesse preempted. "Apparently, a lot of them don't have anything to eat."

The television set was on in the living room, tuned to the news with the sound turned down too low to hear. When the broadcast cut to a Salvo commercial, Peter's attention swung from the screen to my face.

"Mr. Dawson," he said.

He appeared to have cleaned himself up since the last time I'd seen him. He wore a button-down shirt with a wide collar and printed with flowers, and looked like he'd even attempted to press it.

"Where's your friend?" I asked him.

"Taking a shower."

Peter pointed a finger behind me.

I turned to see Sly emerge from Cricket's room, shirtless and barefoot, clad only in a pair of tight bell-bottomed trousers with vertical stripes. He was drying his mop of long curls with a bath towel and nodded a wordless acknowledgment of my presence as he twisted past me to open the refrigerator and examine its contents.

I shot a glance at Jesse that said *What the hell?* to which she replied with a wink and a look of amusement.

"I don't mean to be rude, Peter, but what's wrong with the shower at your place?"

"We were staying at that motel down on Route 70, but the bikers kinda took over and asked us to leave."

"They asked you to leave?"

He popped a stray piece of cheese in his mouth and nodded as if this was an everyday occurrence.

"They really didn't have to ask," he said. "It was pretty apparent we weren't welcome."

"So you drove to my house."

Sly was helping himself to a glass of orange juice that he poured from a pitcher he had removed from the refrigerator.

"Cricket said you'd be cool with it."

Before I could say anything that might embarrass her, Cricket changed the subject.

"Peter and Sly said that things were starting to get sketchy down there. No water, no food, no bathrooms."

"I bet there's a thousand people by now," Peter added. "It's radical."

Jesse handed me a steaming mug and leaned a hip on the counter beside me.

"I told Cricket I'd speak with Pastor Dunn from the church to arrange a relief committee," Jesse told me. "He's already got half the congregation making sandwiches and taking contributions for bottles of water and fresh fruit."

"We're delivering it there in the morning," Cricket said.

"Peterson Construction is donating chemical toilets," Jesse put in.

"Tomorrow is Easter," I said.

"When better," Cricket said simply. "Are you going to pitch in here, or what?"

Jesse handed me a roll of cellophane wrap that she drew from one of the brown paper sacks on the counter and I tried to make myself useful.

I listened without comment while Peter and my daughter swapped stories of protests and politics, and came to understand that the mood at Teresa Pineu's had grown decidedly more militant over the past day or so. Hundreds of new demonstrators had been drawn in by news coverage and were now planning a sit-in to block the BLM access road. I held my tongue while they congratulated themselves on their youthful resolve, and on getting the whole thing on film, and knew it was time for me to intercede with the local authorities at land management.

"I don't mean to rain on your campfire," I said. "But you're dealing with a federal agency. You are aware of that, right?"

"Let 'em come," Peter said.

"You need to be careful with that line of thinking. When they do come, they'll be carrying handcuffs and weapons."

"And jackboots and clubs," Cricket said.

I felt a blade of heat cross my face, and reminded myself to remain calm.

"Let me explain how this works," I said. "BLM doesn't have an enforcement arm of its own, so they rely on local officials at first. Right now, that's me."

"So?"

"If they decide I'm not getting the job done to their satisfaction, they call in the staties, or more likely, the National Guard. You remember Kent State?"

"Don't lecture me," she said. "Two days ago, I heard gunfire at Wounded Knee."

"I'm not taking their side, damn it," I said. "The way the bureau's handled the mustangs has been seriously screwed up. You're not in the wrong about that. But I know how this situation plays out if you push them too far. You've got to resolve this through channels. I swear to God, Cricket, I don't want to see you get hurt. I don't want to see anyone get hurt over this."

She shook her head in frustration and pushed away from the table.

"Let's box this stuff up," she said to Peter.

I heard a knock at the front door, rinsed my hands in the sink, and dried them on a dish towel before I went to answer it. I could feel my daughter bore holes in my back with her stare.

Jordan Powell and Samuel Griffin stood on the porch, eyes locked onto the floorboards and trying to give the appearance that they hadn't heard the raised voices inside.

"Sorry to interrupt," Samuel said.

"What can I do for you boys?"

"Captain," Powell said. "Me and Griffin want to volunteer. I know you said to sleep on it, but I done all the thinking I need to."

"That goes for me too, Mr. Dawson."

I looked into their faces and measured the expressions they wore. They were two of my very best, and they'd both had military experience. I would have selected them myself had it not been beyond any appropriate expectation, and I was humbled to a point that choked me for words.

"I appreciate that more than you know," I said.

Powell nodded and moved toward the stairway, but Griffin stayed put, twisting the brim of the hat in his hand and studied on thoughts I could see roiling behind his eyes.

I didn't trust myself to speak any further, so turned to go back in the house.

I was stopped in my tracks by a firm grip on my shoulder.

"There's something you need to know, Mr. Dawson," Samuel said. The tone of his voice was low, confidential, but his firmness of purpose was fixed in his eyes.

"Nobody's expecting miracles from you, sir," he whispered. "You don't have nail wounds in your hands."

—*∞*—

I STRODE to the office to place the phone call to Melissa Vernon at the BLM office in Salem. They put my call through right away.

"I know this is a Saturday . . ."

"Is that a dig of some kind, Mr. Dawson?" she said. "A statement on the efficacy of the federal government?"

"I am unfamiliar with the working hours of the bureau."

"We're running out of patience with Teresa Pineu."

"Is that an ultimatum of some kind, Ms. Vernon?"

The clack of typewriters and a flurry of voices filled the empty space on her end of the connection.

"You may infer whatever you like."

"We need to talk, Ms. Vernon," I said.

"You can make an app—"

"That won't work for me. We need to talk *now*."

PART THREE:
TROUBLE

CHAPTER THIRTEEN

EASTER MORNING BROKE boldly, a bank of cumulus stacked up along the back range, illuminated from within as though painted with the muscular brush strokes of the masters.

Peter Davis had not overestimated the size of the crowd that had assembled on Teresa Pineu's property, nor the aura of militancy and the portent of violence it had come to exude. They had constructed a makeshift dais from wood pallets and upturned produce crates, where an unidentified woman now stood speaking into an amplified megaphone. I could not hear the words at this distance, but the cadence and tone put me in mind of a tin pot dictator.

I had parked at a far corner of a neighboring property whose fields were clotted with uprooted stones and clumps of dry weeds. Jordan Powell pulled his truck in beside mine, and both he and Samuel Griffin got out as I stood waiting with one hand resting on my hood. Teresa Pineu had seen us arrive and was crossing the open ground at a jog.

"I'm happy to see you," she said. Her breathing was labored from the distance she'd run; loose skin around her eyes was puffed and dry from lack of sleep. It was not the reception I had expected.

I introduced her to Jordan and Sam, whom she acknowledged with the briefest of nods before returning her attention to me. A white pinfeather was lodged in the dark curls of her hair and fluttered in a ripple of wind.

"You've got something stuck here," I said and plucked it out for her.

"I was feeding the chickens when I saw you drive up."

"Looks like you got what you wanted," I said as my eyes roved over the spreading sea of supporters and the encampment they'd created.

"I don't know where they all came from," she said, and looked away from me toward the hills. "You warned me about this."

"You knew it was coming, Teresa."

"Not like this."

"Have the Charlatans been back?"

"They ride through every day. I'm sure they're selling dope, and they like the young girls."

"Have you seen this one?"

In the office the night before, I'd made mimeographed copies of the photo Emily Meeghan's father had given me. I showed one to Teresa Pineu.

"I don't think so," she said. "It's hard to say."

The stannic bleat of the megaphone went silent, and the young woman stepped down from the stage and cast a glance in our direction. Her mane of unruly curls was like an aura, backlit by the sun. She was replaced a few seconds later by a rangy kid in dungarees and a chambray shirt with sleeves rolled up beyond his elbows, looking like he had just been furloughed out from Parchman Farm. He took a seat on an upturned apple crate and started strumming Woody Guthrie songs on a guitar.

Griffin and Powell wore serious expressions that betrayed their bewilderment and discomfiture with respect to both the size and semblance of the gathering. The mood now hovered somewhere between a rock concert and antiwar rally. The earlier arrivals had embraced a more pacifistic and egalitarian inclination, while the newer ones seemed to possess a distinctly more agitated mind-set. My main concern was not with this group as it was, its magnitude notwithstanding, but the delicate chemistry that could easily ignite if indelicately prodded or intentionally primed by outside influences, whether deployed by the authorities or otherwise.

"It's beginning to sound like a Weather Underground meeting," I said.

"All I was trying to do was save the horses," she said.

"I spoke with land management yesterday."

"Melissa Vernon?"

I nodded.

"You're embarrassing her," I said. "And the bureau's scared of what's happening out here."

"And you're supposed to make it all go away."

"May I speak bluntly?"

"Please."

"If this lasts too much longer, they will bring people in from outside. Bureaucrats have a low threshold of tolerance for embarrassment."

"What are you saying to me?"

"You've made your point clear to them, Teresa. It's time to go speak with Ms. Vernon. I believe she will listen to you now. But if this situation makes one wrong turn, that window's going to close down on you. And when it does, it's going to close down on you hard."

EARLIER THAT morning, in the near dark of predawn, Pastor
Dunn, Jesse, Cricket, and at least fifty other members of our
church's congregation had erected a pavilion: a cluster of tent-
covered tables where food, bottled water, and baskets of fresh
fruit were being dispensed into the hands of young people
who had begun to form lines along the periphery. Teresa used
the megaphone to announce their presence from her position
on the platform, and the bleary-eyed faces of hippies, freaks,
and activists peeked out from the openings of tipis, lean-tos,
and VW buses, and tents made of sailcloth and reclaimed
canvas. They emerged wrapped in warm coats if they had
them, or with shoulders draped with wrinkled blankets and
hand-sewn quilts to straggle across the untilled rocky soil to
find a place in line. I heard no discussion or mention con-
cerning religion, not even from the pastor, only watched as
the distribution took place with a quiet efficiency I never
would have imagined.

An hour later the tables were bare, the food consumed
while church volunteers busied themselves with the striking
of tents, disassembling of tables, and loading all the parts and
pieces into the cargo hold of a military surplus flatbed truck.
The sun rose over the peaks of the mountains as the clouds
scudded away to the north, propelled by a high-altitude current. Down here on the ground, the air remained still and the
smell of the wood smoke from slash piles mingled with that
of fresh culms of wild rye and foxtail.

The climate of amorphous agitation that defined the atmosphere just a short time earlier had diffused into one of community. The televised riots and outbursts of violence that had
become a staple of nightly news broadcasts had done a disser-
vice to the notion of lawful protest, and created the impression that an entire generation of youth was hell-bent on little
more than pointless destruction and the dismemberment of

the world as we knew it. While it would be naive not to recognize the existence of those whose interests were to incite and
disseminate doctrines of nihilism and anarchy, the vast major-
ity of those who had gathered in support of Teresa Pineu and
the mustangs were nothing of the sort.

I could see that these kids had been raised to believe in the
System, but had come to understand, through either personal
experience or observation of current events, that the system
had begun to corrode, perverted by a caste of career politi-
cians who viewed their world in terms of demographic groups
and core constituencies, and that the voices that expected to
be heard from inside the voting booth had the same social
significance and value as the contents of a colostomy bag.

When had the role of government begun to devolve from
a mind-set of public service to one in which it was acceptable
to apply the use of outright force to coerce compliance from
its citizens? I wanted no part in that practice.

I searched for Cricket among the church volunteers, and
finally found her loading tent poles on the flatbed with the
help of Powell and Griffin.

"You did a good thing for these people, Cricket," I said.
"I'm proud of you. I want you to know that."

She looked at me for a long moment before she answered,
clearly nursing remnants of hostility from our conversation
the day before.

"It's the least that we could do before you haul them off
to jail," she said.

"I don't think you understand my intentions here."

She shook her head and I could see the hurt crowding
her eyes.

"I need to get back to work," she said, and walked away.

A dust devil spun up from the open field, then disappeared
into a patch of weeds. I motioned to Powell and Griffin and

they followed me a small distance away, out of earshot of the crowd.

"This would be a good time to circulate," I said. "While everybody's eating."

I divided a sheaf of mimeographed photos into three piles, passed one to each of the men and kept the last one for myself.

I threaded my way between the tents and tipis, stopping off at each, receiving only shrugs and shaking heads in reply when asked if anyone had seen Emily Meeghan. I spotted Teresa Pineu near the improvised stage, in what appeared to be a heated exchange with the curly headed speechmaker who had earlier been so intent on inciting outrage in the crowd.

Teresa shook her head in frustration and stalked over to meet me.

"When I speak with that woman I feel like I'm pushing on a string."

"Would you mind if I said a few words?"

Teresa stepped up on the boards and called for attention. She introduced me as the local law, which drew a predictable wave of catcalls and hoots, but when she pleaded for their silence they eventually complied.

I hoisted a copy of the photo of Emily Meeghan above my head and did my best to appeal for their assistance in helping us locate her. I pledged that my interest in her was not motivated by anything other than the confirmation of her well-being and to put her father's mind at ease. My announcement was met with a frustrating combination of disinterest and distrust, and I folded the paper photo into the pocket of my coat.

I took a moment to scan the crowd, who were spread out in every direction, seated cross-legged on beach towels and tarps, some standing or milling along the perimeter. From my vantage point four feet off the ground, I noticed for the first time that several dozen demonstrators sat with their arms interlaced in such a way as to completely block the right-of-way that granted access to the contested BLM land. Some distance beyond them, in the direction of the state road, I also saw two unmarked vehicles parked some distance farther on. They bristled with radio antennae and gave the distinct impression that they were occupied by officers or agents who had been granted authority to impose martial law. It was a blatant violation of the understanding I thought I'd worked out with Melissa Vernon, and white heat flashed through my veins. This is how it invariably begins.

I pressed the toggle on the megaphone and spoke once again to the group.

"I've been in contact with the Bureau of Land Management," I said. "And this is what they had to say: Their policy is to rely on local law enforcement to disperse you from this property . . ."

My words were drowned out in a cacophony of jeers and profanity, and I waited for it to die away.

"I have been urged in no uncertain terms to do exactly that. Should I fail to disperse you, I am told they will likely involve the National Guard, and I have no desire to see that happen. I remember the massacre at Kent State, and I know you do too. A repeat of that tragedy is not acceptable."

Off to my right, Teresa Pineu stood watching me with an expression of incredulity, believing that I had betrayed her.

"Let me tell you where I stand."

The uneasy silence felt like a barometric shift, as though my next words could ignite a combustible outburst without further warning or provocation.

"As far as I am concerned, the Constitution granted every one of you the right to assemble peacefully. If Teresa Pineu has no objection to your presence on her property, than neither do I.

"It also says you have the right to speak your mind, and the right to protest policies that you find objectionable, provided that you do no harm in the process."

I glanced again at Teresa, whose face had broken into a smile.

"I've seen no harm done here," I said. "And as long as that remains the case, you have my support to continue."

Teresa looked at me and mimed the words, *thank you*.

"I urge you to maintain an attitude of peace. You have earned the attention of the BLM. Now it's up to Teresa Pineu to sit down with the authorities and negotiate a proper freedom for the wild horses that roam on public land.

"That land belongs to you, to me, and all of us. Use your voices, and please, please do not allow yourselves to be manipulated into acting with violence. Do not allow your passion to be exploited here, by *anyone*.

"That's all I have to say."

I stepped down from the rostrum while the atmosphere remained enveloped in stunned silence. A single pair of hands began to clap, and then another and another, until the whole group rose to their feet.

Twin trails of dust clouds arose from behind me as the unmarked vehicles executed U-turns and sped back toward the highway. I handed Teresa the bullhorn, her face a mask of mute amazement.

"It's up to you now," I said. "Go speak with Melissa Vernon, and do it soon. There's not much time left on the clock."

———

PETER DAVIS was the first person to reach me, weaving his way through the milling mass of humanity.

He pulled me off to one side and turned his back toward the crowd. Sly stepped up beside him, camera rolling as always. Peter's expression put me in mind of a cat about to lay a trophy on my doormat.

"Turn that fucking thing off," Peter hissed in Sly's direction.

Sly appeared confused but did what he was told.

"There's some people over there that think they saw her," Peter said.

"Saw who? Emily?"

"Yeah."

"Which people?"

"I promised I wouldn't say."

"I need to speak with them."

"No offense, man, but these folks really don't like talking to the pigs."

"You're suggesting I should take no offense when you refer to me as a pig?"

"You know what I mean."

"I'm trying to like you, Peter, but you don't make it easy."

He showed me a lopsided grin, and shrugged as if there was nothing he could do about what I'd said.

"Where is she?"

"I don't know exactly, but they're pretty sure she rode off with a couple of the biker dudes."

"Please tell me you're making a bad joke."

He shook his head.

"Did she leave with them willingly?"

"I didn't ask, man."

"Any idea where they went?"

"No, but there's still a bunch of 'em hanging out at the motel."

There was only one motel at this end of the valley, so I didn't need to ask which one he meant.

"I appreciate your help, Peter."

He put his hands in the air as if I'd threatened to arrest him.

"You didn't hear a thing from me, man."

"If it makes you feel any better, that's not very far from the truth," I said. "And put your goddamned hands down."

I walked away in search of Cricket, wanted badly to clear the air with her, but was told she had left some time ago.

CHAPTER FOURTEEN

THE CAYUSE MOTEL stood alone on a long, empty stretch of the old state route that had been largely abandoned by motorists since the completion of the interstate. The motel itself had been left in disrepair long before the advent of the freeway, and I couldn't imagine the local Indian tribe for which it was named would have taken much pride in their namesake.

I saw Griffin and Powell's vehicle in my rearview as I approached the turnout, and the silhouette outlines of the three long guns—two Winchester carbines and a pump-action shotgun—that hung in the rack affixed inside Powell's rear window. Loose stones from the gravel of the unpaved lot pinged along the undercarriage of my truck and I momentarily lost my two cowboys inside a gray cloud of loose dirt.

I pulled to a stop in front of a single-story structure constructed of concrete block painted over in sun-faded pink, and laid out in the shape of an L. The short end was comprised of an office and apartment for the manager, the rooms laid out on the long end. A freestanding structure of the same construction and vintage that had once been a Flying A station stood abandoned on the opposite corner, loose tar-paper shingles flapping listlessly in the breeze.

Near the door to the office, a handwritten sign had been taped to a window filmed by a layer of brown dust and fly-specks. The words No Vacancy were printed on it with a black felt-tip marker.

I stepped down from my pickup and walked toward the office, counting five motorcycles parked side by side outside the long row of rooms. I tried the handle, but the door wouldn't open. I pounded my fist on the jamb until a light fixture switched on over the desk inside, and an elderly man with a sunken chest and bald head shuffled over and glared at me through a half-opened jalousie.

"We're closed," he said from the other side of the glass.

His left eye had been blackened and a knot the size of a walnut had swelled to the point that the skin split open and stood out on the crown of his skull.

"Sheriff's office," I said. "Open up."

"I don't want any dealings with you."

"Most people don't. Open the door."

The sound of crunching gravel closed in from behind, and I turned to see Peter Davis's piss-yellow van slide to a stop beneath a reader board sign that was framed in the shape of an Indian headdress. At one time the letters had been arranged to advertise the promise of free telephone and TV, but several had been damaged or fallen away long since.

I moved from the manager's office and came up beside the driver's side of the van and waited while Peter cranked down his window.

"What are you doing?" I asked him.

"Following you."

"I can see that. Go home."

"This is all part of the story, man."

The ashen-faced manager reappeared at the doorway wearing a pair of loose-fitting chinos belted high over his stomach and waving his arms over his head in exasperation.

"I told you two to get out of here," he hollered at Peter.

"See?" Peter said to me. "What'd I tell you?"

"Stay in the van," I said, and knew damn well he wouldn't.

"What happened to your head?" I asked the old man.

"They happened," he said, gesturing toward the row of Harleys tilted at an angle on their kickstands.

"They assaulted you?"

"What the hell do you think? There ain't any stairs around here to fall down from."

"How many of them?"

"How many what?"

"What have we been talking about? How many god-damned bikers are here?"

"Eight or nine, maybe."

"I only count five bikes."

"A few of 'em left."

"When?"

"Not long ago," he said. "I don't really keep track of their comings and goings."

"What did they look like?"

"What do any of 'em look like? One had a helmet like a Wehrmacht soldier, two looked like pirates, and the last idiot had his foot wrapped up in a bandage."

Peter and Sly had crept up on my right flank while I'd been talking, and were committing the entire conversation to film.

"Would you two please give me some room?" I said.

They backed up three paces and kept rolling.

"Which rooms do they occupy?" I said to the old man.

"Dig the manure out of your ears, son," he said, shaking his head at the obtuseness of my question. "All of 'em."

Heat shimmers rose up from the parking lot as I looked across. Three Charlatans in full road regalia had exited their rooms and stood beside the row of bikes, arms chained with blue tattoos crossed upon their chests.

"I'm going back inside," the manager said. "And I'm locking the door behind me. Don't come back unless it's to tell me you caged those gorillas. I'm done."

I made a circling gesture in the air above my head and pointed at Jordan Powell still sitting behind the wheel of his idling truck.

"Follow me."

We drove the short distance across the lot, parked close behind the line of Harleys and blocked them in. Powell and Griffin stepped out of the cab, removed the carbines cradled in the gun rack while I unshipped my Colt from its holster.

"Afternoon, fellas," I said.

The largest of the group stepped forward, hooked his thumbs inside a leather belt strung with a knife sheath and a length of metal chain that looped along his hip.

"You looking for someone?"

"Might be," I said. "Who've you got?"

He grinned and glanced in Samuel Griffin's direction.

"You brought your nigger with you this time," he said. "How nice for you."

"That's not a term that gets used in my presence," I said. "You do not want to utter it again."

"I was trying to compliment you, Sheriff, on your affirmative action hire."

Powell cocked the lever on his rifle, tucked the stock into his shoulder, and sighted down the barrel.

I addressed Samuel without taking my eyes off of the biker.

"Sam, you have my permission to chain drag this man across the parking lot if he makes one more racist remark."

The squeal of a rusted door hinge caught my attention, and a bearded face peered out through the opening, the security chain stretched tight, still fastened to the wall. Powell swiveled and drew a bead on it.

"Get back inside, or this man will open fire," I said.

Beard made a grab for the chain lock, and Powell splintered the frame with a .30-caliber slug. The door slammed shut as a whiff of smoke drifted from the mouth of Powell's barrel and the odor of spent powder filled the air. He jacked the lever and a brass jacket arched into the gravel.

"You got a name?" I asked.

"Fuck off," the big one answered.

He sucked on a wood matchstick he drew from his vest pocket, and rolled it across his teeth.

"I've got to call you something if we're going to engage in conversation," I said. "I think I'll call you 'Wallace.' You seem to share the governor's views on racial matters. He's in a wheelchair now."

Griffin thumbed back his hammer. This situation was escalating with the rapidity and lethality of a prison riot. In my peripheral vision I saw Sly and Peter moving sideways in a slow arc behind us, filming the scene as if they had scripted it, as if they were immune from harm.

"Back the hell off, Peter," I said. "I mean it."

I dipped two fingers into the pocket of my shirt and shook the folds out of the photo of Emily Meeghan.

"Have you seen this girl, Wallace?"

He slid a pair of mirrored shades from his face and made a show of examining the picture.

"Can't say for sure," he said. "Gash all tends to look the same to me after a while."

An ambiguous thought had been troubling me for some time, but I could not put a name to it until now. The man I called 'Wallace' had eyes that were lit up from inside like he was plugged into a wall socket, and the planes of his face twitched with the static electrical buzz of the amphetamines that surged through his bloodstream. But there was some other agenda operating inside his head. The collective IQ of his companions wouldn't break double digits, and it was clear to me that he was in charge. Now the thing that had been troubling me had begun to take form, and I wondered where the rest of the Charlatans were. Lloyd Skadden had been warned of a massive rally of outlaws, yet I had only encountered this small band.

"I believe this girl is here with you now," I said. "Care to study on the picture again?"

He passed it back to me without a glance, adjusting his scrotum with his free hand.

"Now that you mention it, she does look familiar."

I felt the rough crosshatch press into my palms as I gripped the Colt tight in my fist.

"I'm going to ask you this only two times," I said. "The first time is going to be polite: Is she inside that room behind you?"

He smiled and shifted his weight to the balls of his feet. Griffin and Powell saw it too.

"I think she's grown fond of the attention she enjoys from the boys," Wallace said. The two standing beside him broke into grins. "Although she was a little hesitant at first."

"You'll need to stand aside," I said. "All three of you. Hands out to your sides, palms out."

They complied, and I patted them down for weapons. None carried firearms, but the collection of fighting blades was impressive. I tossed the entire haul of boot knives, karambits, and switchblades into the bed of my truck. Then I came back for the ignition keys to their Harleys and slid them into my pocket.

"You got a warrant?" Wallace asked me.

"I've got a boot-heel warrant," I said. "Would you like to take a closer look?"

Griffin and Powell moved toward the men, the carbine stocks still tucked in tight at their jawlines. The two cowboys loose-herded the bikers into the shade of the motel's roof overhang and lined them up along the wall. The grins had disappeared from their faces.

"Do you see the guns these men are directing at you?" I said. "They're Winchester model 94 repeating rifles. They fire .30-caliber bullets that will pass through your internal organs and leave a hole on the way out that's the size of my fist. There are eight rounds in each chamber, so there's fifteen left. If you can't do the arithmetic in your heads, it works out like this: Five holes apiece. At this distance, I guarantee that these men will not miss."

I moved toward the locked door of the room at their backs, felt the knurled surface of the hammer of the Colt against my thumb, and cocked it. I reeled back and planted a solid kick beside the handle, and the door gave way in a shower of chipped pressboard and plaster dust, ripped the chain from the anchor bolts, slammed open, and bounced against the wall.

I shouldered past the threshold and into the darkened room, illuminated only by a narrow strip of daylight where the cheap vinyl curtains had parted and the rectangle of light that now shone through the shattered doorway. One Charlatan stood at the side of a filthy and disheveled bed holding a Polaroid camera, a bandana tied tight across his brow. He had been snapping images of his porcine companion as he thrust himself between the upraised knees of a female whose face I could not see, his road-soiled jeans and underwear pulled down and pooled around his boots. The fat rapist rolled off the girl and gaped into the black tunnel of the Colt's barrel, his eyes wild and unfocused and deranged with rut. The warning shot that Powell had planted in the doorway hadn't been enough to distract them from their recreation.

The room was dense with the raw, glandular odors of copulation and sweat and a charred, pungent chemical smell I could not identify. The girl on the bed lay battered and prone, immobilized, one wrist shackled to the bed frame with a pair of steel handcuffs. Her face and chest were marbled with bruises, her abdomen spattered with drops of perspiration and dried semen and the blistered scars from burning cigarettes.

She stirred and tried to sit upright, but was caught short by her manacles. Despite the dimness of the light and the physical damage inflicted on her face, I knew without a doubt that I had found Emily Meeghan.

The biker wearing the bandana bounced the Polaroid off the mattress and made a swift turn on me, a push-knife locked inside his fist. I held the Colt in a two-handed stance and stared down the sight and into his jangling eyes.

"I will drop you where you stand," I said. "I shit you not."

The twin edges of the blade reflected in the band of light that streamed in between the curtains and he moved it slowly back and forth, like the searching head of a snake.

I cocked the hammer on the Colt, and the ratchet of the mechanism snapping home appeared to awaken him from a trance.

"Last chance," I said. "Drop it on the floor."

I tried to whistle for Powell, but my mouth had gone bone dry, and I fought the urge to empty my entire cylinder into this guy's bandana. I hollered out for Powell instead, and the biker dropped his blade. The fat rapist had slid off the bed and onto the floor where he was struggling to pull his pants up over his pink and pockmarked buttocks.

Powell appeared in the doorway and leveled his rifle at the half-naked man on the floor. Together, we directed them to kneel on the carpet and press their palms flat to the wall. I relieved them of their knife blades and keys, then went to unlock the cuffs that still bound Emily Meeghan.

She rubbed the raw red indentations where the cuffs had bitten into her wrists and passed a vacant gaze over the room. I had seen the look before, in the eyes of combat veterans and the victims of sudden and unspeakable horrors.

Powell covered the bikers while I handcuffed the rapist then stepped outside to collect ropes from the cabs of our trucks.

"Get down on your faces," I said and went to work hog-tying them both. I looped a second length of rope around a single leg of each man, securing each one to the other.

When I was finished, I hoisted them to their feet and herded them outdoors, hobbling like drunks in a three-legged race, and tossed them facedown into the bed of Powell's pickup.

I stepped up beside Samuel Griffin while Powell finished anchoring the two captives to the cargo hooks of the truck.

Fat beads of sweat had popped out on Samuel's forehead and darkened the seam of his hatband. His Winchester was leveled at Wallace's chest, and when I looked at Sam's face, he gave me a wink that told me he still had things under control.

Fear has an odor, like vinegar and sweat and milk that's gone sour in the bottle. Despite the façade of bravado, it clung to the three bikers like a second skin.

I uncocked the Colt and breathed a deep breath, slid the gun inside my holster. The engraved scrollwork on the frame and barrel was a hallmark of my grandfather's time, when men such as these would have been bounced off the limb of a tree. I thought he might well be looking down upon me now, with disgust and contempt at my cowardice in not having done exactly that already.

I returned to the motel room and helped Emily cover herself with a bedsheet, averting my eyes out of respect and the deep-seated shame for the barbarity she had endured at the subhuman hands of the worst examples of my gender. She hadn't spoken a word, and neither had I as I carried her outside and lifted her into the passenger seat of my truck. Sly and Peter sidled up behind me, their distorted images reflecting off the curvature of the windshield.

"What the hell is the matter with you?" I said. "You get out of this girl's face with that thing."

I took the five sets of keys I had liberated from the Charlatans and walked to the edge of the parking lot. Across the paved road, the forest was dense, impacted, and choked with a tangle of wild berries, thistle sage, and nettle. One by one, I pitched each set into the bramble, where I knew it would take hours to find them, if they ever did find them at all.

CHAPTER FIFTEEN

THE PHONE CORD had been ripped from the wall in the room where Emily Meeghan had been held captive, so I called Jesse from the motel office. I gave her only the most minimal of details, but asked that she get in touch with Emily's father to have him meet me at the substation in Meridian.

The manager complained bitterly about the damage that had been done to his motel, without a word or question in regard to the abused young girl who sat waiting for me, wrapped in a filthy sheet and blanket, in the cab of my idling truck. I suggested he send a bill for the damage to Charlatans' headquarters in San Bernardino and left him in the office, shouting a string of obscenities and threats at my retreating back.

Emily was shivering, catatonic, and suspended inside a haze of thoughts that I could only guess at. Her bare feet rested on the seat cushion, arms encircling her knees, drawn up into a trembling fetal ball. She stared, unblinkingly at the fading light of afternoon, disappearing right before my eyes, neither living nor yet dead, hovering somewhere in between and wedged into the farthest corner of my truck.

We drove the state route north in silence, Powell and Griffin in my rearview, accompanied only by the whisper of the

road beneath my wheels. Half an hour later, we turned onto
the county road and passed through mile after mile of wood-
land blanketed in cattail moss and broken stumps of hemlock
overgrown by wild mushrooms. A deer trail switched back
through the forest into a barren clear-cut where raw logs and
rough timber had been hauled off to pulp and lumber mills
chained to the beds of stinger trucks.

Emily had given in to sleep, her head rocking gently where
it rested against the window. I switched on my headlights, lit
a cigarette, and made a mental catalog of the anguish I would
like to bring to bear on any man who would do what had
been done to her.

—————

THERE WAS a private entrance to the Meridian substation
at the rear of the building, but the sodium lamp back there
was dead and the lot was far too dark. The main street was
practically deserted, so we parked along the curb outside the
front door instead.

Chandle Meeghan paced back and forth within the pool
of pinkish light beneath the lamppost, his hands buried deep
in the pockets of his coat, and I could hear him muttering
to himself. Emily's eyelids fluttered as she came slowly awake,
then her eyes filled with tears and something else when they
fell upon her dad.

"I'm sorry, Chandle," I said. "But she needs to see a doctor,
and this is the quickest way to get her to one."

"Is she all right?"

He moved stiffly, his expression dazed and empty, like a
man suddenly awakened from deep sleep.

"Bring your car around, and I'll help put her inside."

I unlocked the door to the substation and snapped on the
overhead lights. Griffin untied the prisoners, dragged the taller

one from the rear of his truck and onto his feet then prodded him into the precinct.

Yellow headlights rounded the corner and Chandle pulled up to the curb. He held open his passenger door while I carried Emily from my cab and placed her gently on the seat of Chandle's car. Her body felt limp and weightless and she had begun trembling again. Chandle pushed on his door until the mechanism clicked shut, taking care not to slam it and break the fragile quiet.

By this time, the fat rapist had been dragged out of Powell's truck bed, his boot soles shuffling on the sidewalk, still tightly bound at the ankles and wrists, the barrel of Powell's carbine pressed into the hollow of his back.

"Is this the man who hurt my daughter?" he asked me.

"Please step away, Mr. Meeghan."

"Is this him?"

Meeghan moved up on the sidewalk and blocked Powell's path. Without warning, he swung on the biker and landed a crushing blow to the bridge of his nose. A spatter of blood caught the light and arced onto the front of Chandle Meeghan's collared shirt. I could tell that the man had likely never been in a fistfight, nor properly taught how to throw a punch. He cocked back again for another, and Powell made a move to prevent it, but I shook my head.

I allowed Meeghan to unleash his rage, exhausting himself with three more body blows. Blood from the biker's ruptured septum dripped in a free-flowing sheet off his chin. He showed Meeghan a smile stained in pink, leaned toward him, and spat blood in his face.

Powell reacted with a swift stroke from the butt of his carbine that cracked off a front tooth along the gumline. The broken tooth fell to the ground and Meeghan smeared a pink streak of spittle across his face with the back of his hand. His eyes filled with the scalding tears of impotence.

Meeghan's chest heaved and we both watched in silence as Powell frog-marched the prisoner inside and kicked the door shut behind him.

"Take Emily to County General," I told Meeghan. "We've got this now."

———

WE LOCKED the prisoners in two of the three separate cells upstairs, and I left Powell to keep an eye on them for a while. Griffin and I took seats at the desks on the first floor.

"What happens now, Mr. Dawson?" Griffin asked me, but I had no answer.

I phoned the diner and ordered some food while Griffin set about searching the office for any equipment that might have been left in the lockers. When I hung up, I ran my finger down the typewritten list of telephone numbers that had been tacked on the wall beside the phone and landed on one belonging to the district attorney's office. This being Easter Sunday, I figured they'd be closed, but I dialed it anyway and left a message with the answering service.

I called Jesse next and told her I wouldn't be home that night.

"Is Emily okay?" Jesse asked.

"Not even close."

"And you?"

"I'll be fine," I said. "Keep Wyatt inside with you, and make sure all the doors are locked. There's a .38 in the night-stand. I want you to keep it underneath your pillow."

"What's happening, Ty?"

"Please tell me you'll do what I asked."

Griffin was making a racket as he rifled the cabinets and drawers, so I plugged one ear with my finger and listened to Jesse breathing on the other end of the line. I told her I loved her, and placed one final call. This one was to Caleb Wheeler.

"I found some stuff," Griffin said when I'd finished my call to Caleb. He crossed the room carrying an armload of the crap he'd found, and dumped it on my desk.

We picked through a tangle of batteries, chargers, and the cables that went with a set of handheld radios. They looked to be at least ten years old, and had likely been left there because they either were broken or never had functioned properly at any distance in this valley. I had some unfortunate experience with equipment much like this when I was in Korea.

"Plug 'em into the wall and let's see if they work," I said. "What else did you find?"

"Two pairs of handcuffs and an old billy club."

"That's it?"

"The rest is just papers and outdated phone books," he said. "What's that smell in here, anyway?"

"Dysfunction."

Tiny red lights glowed on the chargers that Griffin plugged into the wall. We sat in silence and watched them blink and listened to Powell tap his boots on the floor overhead.

A face appeared in the sidelight window next to the door. Rowan Boyle's breath fogged the glass as he cupped a hand to his cheekbone and peered inside. I could see the shadows of two others right behind him.

"It takes three of you to deliver sandwiches?" I asked, as I turned the key in the lock and let them inside.

Boyle set a cardboard box in the space Griffin had cleared on the bookcase. I peered inside at a plate stacked with a dozen sandwiches he'd cut in half and covered with waxed paper. Ribbons of steam drifted up from lidded paper cups brimming with coffee, tucked tight beside a six-pack of Diet Rite Cola.

Boyle's lips squirmed like he was rehearsing a speech he had memorized, and his companions kept running their eyes toward the stairwell in back.

"Can we get a look at the prisoners?" he asked finally.

"You ever slopped hogs?" I asked.

"Surely have."

"Then there's nothing up there you haven't seen before."

"I thought maybe—"

I shook my head.

"I'm going to need you to take back these cola bottles," I interrupted. "You got something else that comes packaged in cans?"

"I can probably find something."

"I appreciate it," I said and held the door open for them. "Thank you, Rowan."

Powell came down the stairs when they'd gone, and eyed the box on the bookcase.

"You two go ahead and eat," I said.

I took three of the sandwiches upstairs and passed one to each of the bikers through the bars. I sat down to eat mine while I watched them. The room already smelled like a musty barn where rodents had nested in soiled linen, defecated, and died. There was no solvent, bleach, or astringent that could ever be sufficient to scrub the opprobrium from these walls; nothing short of fire ever would.

"This is it?" the tall one asked.

"Shut up and eat."

"I thought these small towns were supposed to be hospitable."

"I told you to shut up."

"I'm thirsty," the rapist lisped.

"Don't care."

I finished off my sandwich and stood at the top of the stairs, turning the light off behind me.

"It's goddamned dark in here."

"You'll see light in the morning," I said. "Consider yourselves lucky. You should be tree decorations by now. Now shut the fuck up."

Powell had a row of brass cartridges lined up on the desk and was running a long-handled bore brush through the barrel of his carbine while Griffin hummed something under his breath and rocked back and forth on his rolling chair. I leaned my back to the wall and stared out the glass at the lighted storefronts along the street.

"You seem awfully calm, Jordan," I said.

He glanced at me for a moment and returned to his work.

"You know how you survive a shit show like 'Nam?" he asked. "You admitted to yourself that if you were there in the first place, you were probably already dead. So, if you're already dead and already in-country, then you might as well make the best of it."

"That's what you think this is?"

"No, Captain," he smiled. "I'm saying I made my peace a long time ago. You know what I mean. You've seen the elephant. There's not much that scares me no more."

My gaze roamed the street and my bones felt like water as the adrenaline leeched out of my bloodstream.

"You got a funny look on your face, Mr. Dawson," Griffin said.

"Just tired."

"You mind if I say something that's none of my business?"

"Here comes the deacon," Powell said.

"What's that supposed to mean?" I asked.

"The boys call me Deacon 'cause I read the bible sometimes before bed."

Powell raised his palms skyward and waggled his fingers.

"I don't bother preaching," Griffin told me. "The savior I serve doesn't need to be forced on nobody. You just got a sad look on your face, is all."

"Go ahead, Griffin," I said. "Speak your mind."

"I don't have children of my own, and I already said I'm no minister. But there's something I believe you need to know."

"What's that, Samuel?"

"God gives us children to teach us humility."

I pulled my eyes off the window and onto his.

"I don't think I'm following this conversation," I said.

"I've seen how it is with you and your daughter. And I saw that poor Mr. Meeghan with his little girl."

"What are you trying to say?"

"How else could God show you how it feels to have somebody you love unconditionally just turn around and tell you to go right straight to hell?"

CHAPTER SIXTEEN

THE SUN DID not appear to rise that morning, simply faded in from dark to light and washed a deep blue cast inside the clouds. I stretched the kinks out of my back and neck from sleeping in a chair, and stepped outside to feel the air that smelled of juniper and piñon.

The street was empty at this hour, and the streetlamps had begun to cycle off. I turned my face into the breeze that swept down from the slopes, chilled but not enough so as to turn my breath to fog. In the distance, slender funnels of white smoke rose up from timber stumps left smoldering in damp soil.

The gables and arcades of frontier architecture etched themselves in stark relief against the lambent sky, and my footsteps echoed on the boards along an old section of sidewalk still inset with posts and iron rings where teams of horses had once been tied. Yellow light warmed the window of the diner and the susurrus of voices spilled outside.

I ordered coffee from the diner's counter and ruminated on my day. The room was rippling with the welcome noise of normalcy, and the muted conversations across laminated table-tops, and speckled china dishware heaped with fried potatoes, eggs, and slabs of ham and buttered toast.

I drank my coffee, ordered egg and cheese sandwiches and cans of orange juice to go while I watched Rowan Boyle through the service window work the flattop flipping pancakes. He nodded when he saw me then focused his attention on the slips of paper clipped to the order carousel. I polished off my coffee when I heard the service bell, paid cash at the register, and carried the box of food back to the station. Across the street, Lankard Downing had nailed a sheet of plywood across the shattered window of the Cotton Blossom, where a painted sign was stapled that said *closed for repairs.*

Griffin sat yawning at his desk when I returned, but Powell was still sacked out on the floor in back between the file cabinets, using his rolled-up jacket as a pillow and a hat to cover his eyes. His Winchester was laid out beside him like a lover. I heard him stir awake when he smelled chow.

I carried some juice and sandwiches to the prisoners upstairs while my cowboys helped themselves. One of the cell toilets had backed up and the air inside the confines of the detention room was heavy with the odor of feces and dried sweat. Without a word, I slid the food across the floor between the bars.

"Somebody needs to fix the shitter," the rapist said.

"I'll call the maid," I said. "Enjoy your meal."

I had just unwrapped my sandwich when my wife and Caleb Wheeler pushed through the front door. She had a thermos and a stack of Styrofoam cups cradled in her arms, and a look on her face that made it clear she was not happy.

"I made Caleb bring me with him," she said to me. "So don't get mad at him."

"I'm not mad at anybody yet," I said. "I asked Caleb to meet me here this morning."

"I know. He told me."

I shot a glance past Jesse's shoulder. Caleb grimaced and shrugged an apology in my direction.

"Good morning, Samuel," she said pleasantly. "Good morning, Jordan."

She set the thermos and the cups beside the food carton on the bookcase while her eyes bored into mine.

"There were armed cowboys on my porch when I woke up this morning," she said. Her tone was phlegmatic and impassive, but her message to me was clear.

"I asked them to look out for you and Cricket," I said.

The ceiling rumbled as the prisoners upstairs began to stomp their feet in unison.

"What is *that*?"

"There's two bikers locked in the cells up there," Powell offered.

"I'll be right back," I said.

The stench hit me in the face again when I reached the landing of the staircase. The rapist was grinning through swollen and scab-crusted lips, his gums and remaining teeth washed in pink from the blood that still seeped from the empty socket in his mouth.

For reasons known only to them, Bandana had attempted to urinate all over the tick mattress on the bunk inside the empty cell. The bed was some distance away, but he had tried anyway, and now most of his stream pooled on the floor.

"Stop pounding your feet," I said.

"We're still hungry," the rapist said.

"Stick your hands outside the bars. Both of you."

When they complied, I cuffed Bandana's left wrist to the rapist's right one, binding them together with a length of iron bar between.

"With your free hand," I said. "Remove your boots and kick them over here to me."

Bandana tried on a mad-dog glare, but I ignored him.

"Do it now," I said. "Or you can spend the rest of the day chained to your cells like that."

I didn't care to handle their soiled footwear, so I left it where it landed.

"Try not to step in your piss," I said.

I unlocked their manacles and went back down the stairs.

"Tell me what's happening, Ty," Jesse said when I returned. Her voice now hovered somewhere between irritation and alarm.

"A gang of bikers called the Charlatans is running off the rails," I said.

"And you didn't think you needed to mention this to me?"

"I thought the situation was under control."

"But you now think they pose a threat to your daughter and your wife," she said. It was a statement, not a question. "This is why armed men were posted on my gallery?"

"I believe it is a possibility," I said. "That's the reason I needed to speak with Caleb this morning."

Jesse crossed her arms protectively and her gaze slipped from my face and out the window. The brittle silence in the room was broken by the ringing of the phone. Powell picked it up before it rang a second time.

"For you," he said and handed the receiver to me.

The person on the other end did not wait for me to announce myself.

"Mr. Dawson, this is Denton Lowell from the district attorney's office."

"Thanks for calling back so early in—"

"Please stop talking," he said. "I understand you have two men in custody for the alleged abduction and forcible rape of Emily Meeghan, is that correct?"

"Yes, I—"

"Let me run some facts by you: You kicked a motel door down without a warrant—"

I am not accustomed to being interrupted, and Denton Lowell had already done it twice. I felt the pulse pound in my temples and an unpleasant heat crawl up my neck.

"Exigent circumstances," I interrupted this time.

"Perhaps," he sighed, impatient, like an overburdened parent. "You also threatened bystanders with bodily harm, and one of your deputies fired a weapon that nearly took a man's face right off his head."

"Care to tell me where the hell this is coming from?" I said. "And for the record, if Jordan Powell had wanted to remove that asshole's face, you would have found it on the wall."

"Charming," Lowell said. "Let me get to the point: Emily Meeghan is refusing to press charges. She insists that her presence with your suspects was entirely of her own volition."

"Lay your eyes on that girl, Mr. Lowell, and tell me she signed on for what she went through. That is complete and utter horseshit."

"I interviewed her at the hospital myself."

"Then someone got to her."

"Kick your prisoners loose, Mr. Dawson, before the county finds itself on the wrong end of a civil suit. Do it today. Do it *now*, in fact."

"That girl was gang raped and burned with cigarettes. Repeatedly."

I was gripping the phone so tightly, my knuckles had gone white.

"Emily Meeghan is free, white, and over eighteen," he said. "She can do as she pleases."

"I don't care for that expression," I said. But I was speaking to a dead connection.

I slammed the receiver into the cradle and turned my eyes on Jesse and Caleb.

"I need you both to leave," I said. "Caleb, take Drambuie and the other horses from the barn and turn them loose up on the North Camp pasture; take the remuda to Three Roses camp and do the same."

"Captain?" Powell said.

"Hold on, Jordan," I said without moving my gaze from Caleb Wheeler's weathered face. "Tell the men to keep one horse apiece and keep them in the sort corral. Anyone who wants to leave right now is free to do so."

"Captain?" Powell said to me again.

"What, goddammit?"

"Look out the window."

Sheriff Skadden had parked his patrol car at the curb and was staring toward the intersection, fists resting on his hips. Five Harleys rumbled into view, driving slowly in formation down the center of the street. I rushed for the door, tossed the station keys to Powell, and told him to lock it behind me once I was outside.

The bikes rolled to a stop and parked at an angle along the curb beside the sheriff's cruiser. The one I had earlier named Wallace hooked a leg over his leather seat and strolled over next to Skadden while the others remained in the saddle.

"Didn't waste any time getting here this morning, Lloyd," I said. "You have a puzzling set of priorities where the execution of your duties is concerned."

"I don't believe in giving a man a responsibility, then turning around and getting in his way."

"No, I surely can't complain that you've been anywhere near my way. You've been practically invisible."

"It's not a training position, Dawson," he smiled and smoothed his mustache with his fingers. "It's like throwing calves. You either tallboy up and get it done, or you don't."

"I appreciate your confidence, Lloyd," I said and turned toward the station. "Have a nice day."

"I understand you've been ordered to let your prisoners go," he said.

"Excuse me?"

Skadden leaned in close enough that I could smell the Vitalis in his hair.

"These fellas are here to pick 'em up," he stage-whispered, then took off his sunglasses and hung them from the top button of his uniform shirt. "I've been asked to supervise their release."

"Wait here," I told him.

"I think we'll just go ahead and wait inside," the sheriff said. I looked at Wallace and he was smiling.

"You'll both wait where I told you to," I said and stepped toward the door again. Inside, Griffin's expression was tense with anticipation. He'd watched the whole exchange from the other side of the glass, one hand tight upon the locking mechanism, the other on his gun.

Wallace squinted toward the station window then turned his eyes on me.

"Is that your wife inside there?" he said. "I'd like to meet her."

"I wonder what I'd find if I tossed your pockets right now, Wallace," I said. "I bet you're carrying half a dozen felonies right there on your person."

"There's no call for that," Skadden interceded. "Everybody settle down."

I studied the sheriff's ruddy face and the clots of red and purple capillaries that had broken on his cheeks. He shoved his hands into his pockets, and rolled his weight along the balls of his feet.

"When a man implies a threat against my wife, I'd say that's cause enough."

"I was only making friendly conversation," Wallace said.

"What gave you the impression we were having a conversation?" I said.

I heard the lock slip as I neared the threshold. Griffin bolted it behind me once I stepped inside again.

"Powell, you come with me," I said. "We have to turn those shitbirds loose."

"Can you repeat that, Captain?" Powell said. "I don't think I heard you right."

"You heard me fine," I said and looked at Caleb Wheeler. "Take Jesse out the back door, and use the long way out of town. Do not drive past those men out front."

I heard Jesse and Caleb leave, and the door click shut behind them, as Powell and I reached the top of the stairs. Griffin waited at the bottom with his rifle at port arms. We cuffed the prisoners behind their backs and marched them back toward the stairwell. No one said a word. We halted at the upstairs landing and I caught the look on Powell's face beside me. I knew what he was thinking, since the same thought had crossed my mind. Nothing would have been as satisfying as to see these two bouncing headfirst down the steps.

"Don't do it," I said softly and shook my head at Powell. "Let's just get this done."

Bandana and the rapist blinked hard against the morning light as Powell and I unchained them. The Charlatans astride their bikes looked on, offering a fanfare of wolf-whistles and applause while my former prisoners rubbed the clefts the ligatures had carved upon their wrists.

"Good Christ," Skadden said, looking at the rapist's broken face. "What the hell happened to this man?"

"He objected to his arrest," I said.

"Looks like he was trampled by the entire Borax mule team."

"It was a vigorous objection."

Wallace took a step in my direction, but Skadden barred his way with an outstretched arm.

"Understandable," Skadden said to me. "Given the man's innocence."

"He's about as innocent as Juan Corona," I said. "Take these two fuck knuckles with you and go. If I see either one of them again, I guarantee you they'll be begging for the rope. That is not an exaggeration."

"That's not a healthy attitude," Wallace said to me.

I ignored him and addressed Lloyd Skadden instead.

"These guys have chewed through the leash," I said. "It's well past time for them to get a bunch of leaving done. I'd recommend they start right now."

CHAPTER SEVENTEEN

JESSE STOOPED OVER the utility tub in the mudroom snipping the ends off the stems of fresh-cut flowers she had collected from the garden. The sunshine through the windowpane cast half her face in shadow and emphasized the highlights in her hair. When she heard me come into the room, she gathered the cuttings into a bouquet of gold daffodils and purple crocus and iris with one hand, the pruning shears still clutched inside the other.

"Come with me to the kitchen," she said, and bussed me on the cheek as she squeezed past me. "I want to put these in a vase."

"Where's Cricket?"

"She went off with Caleb and the boys, moving the horses to Three Roses."

"They left you alone?"

"I can handle myself for a few hours."

She stood on her toes and peered into the pantry.

"I'm sorry about this morning," I said.

"Can you get the green one down for me? I can't reach it."

"Did you hear what I just said?"

"I did, and I am trying to change the subject. Will you please hand me that vase?"

I collected the vase and set it on the counter beside the kitchen sink.

"I can't help from thinking I should be burying those bastards right now."

"Those are not the times we live in, Ty," she said, turned, and leaned her back against the sink.

"I'm tired of feeling like a hypocrite," I admitted. "For a second this morning, I seriously considered shoving a manacled man down a flight of stairs."

"Did you?"

"Did I what?"

"Did you do it?"

"No."

"Because that's not who you are. Yesterday I watched you keep the peace at Teresa Pineu's. A few hours later you rescued a young girl. You didn't deal the cards."

"You didn't see her, Jesse; you didn't see what they did to her. That could have been our daughter."

"Emily Meeghan made bad choices."

"She didn't choose what happened," I said. "I have no interest in judging her decisions."

I had missed it when I'd first come in, walked right past it, but now my attention landed on the shotgun propped up beside the kitchen door. Jesse saw me study it, and something soft came in her eyes.

"Remember when I told you I'd seen the slide," she said. "But I'd never seen it on you?"

"I remember."

"I had no right to say something like that to you."

She stepped into me and wrapped her arms around my waist. She laid her head against my chest and I could smell mulch from the garden and the sunlight on her skin.

"I need to take a shower," I said.

"I'll take one with you."

"I'm ashamed to occupy the same universe as men like that. It'll take a belt sander to scrape the filth off me."

"You can't scare me away," she said, and kissed me gently on the mouth.

"You are a bullheaded woman."

———

I PHONED the hospital after I'd finished dressing, knowing I would not be satisfied until I had spoken with Emily and Chandle Meeghan. After several transfers, I finally spoke with a woman in admissions who informed me that Emily had been released earlier that morning.

I found an address for the Meeghans in the phone book, wrote it down on a sheet of notepaper, and tucked it into the pocket of my vest.

———

A CONTINENTAL Trailways bus was pulling away from the diner as I drove into town, grinding slowly away from the curb and trailing a black cloud of diesel exhaust. Rowan Boyle was smoking a cigarette in the shade of his sidewalk awning, on a lawn chair made of aluminum tubes and plasticized webbing, wearing a T-shirt and stained apron, a paper overseas cap pushed back on his head. He waved a lazy greeting to me as I drove past, and took another deep drag off his smoke.

I made a right turn into a small grid of residential streets that had been given the names of wildflowers. The whole town seemed uncommonly quiet; long afternoon shadows of alder and larch dappled the asphalt and a crosshatch of contrails slashed the sky. The address I'd been looking for was stenciled onto a concrete drainage swale where a moss-crusted brick walkway ran from the street to the front door of a two-story Craftsman. Dim lamplight shone like a damp cotton ball, through lace curtains drawn tight on the casements, the only sounds being those of my footfalls and the creak of a wicker porch swing in a riffle of wind.

I rapped on the doorframe and waited, heard a brief muffled exchange from inside the house. Chandle Meeghan drew a narrow part in the curtains and saw it was me. He stepped to the door, opening it only wide enough to poke his head through.

"I have nothing to say to you," he said.

His face was unshaven and gray, and he still wore the blood-spattered clothes he'd been wearing the night before. The stale, overheated odor of confinement drifted out through the breach and his expression was one of both foreboding and defeat.

"I'm here because I want to help you," I said.

"You can't help me."

"Did someone threaten you or Emily?"

He glanced past my shoulder, up both sides of the street, as if he were expecting to find something there. The tick of the pendulum on the grandfather clock in his foyer echoed on the hardwood floor. He startled visibly when the spring clip suddenly snapped into place and the Westminster chimes sounded the quarter hour.

"Please leave us alone, Dawson. I mean it."

He pushed the door shut as I started to speak, and I heard the deadbolt lock into place.

I cruised the streets of the neighborhood, not knowing what I had expected to find. After nearly an hour, I drove home in silence, haunted by Meeghan's disquiet, and the palpable sensation that I was about to have an arrow parked firmly between the blades of my shoulders.

—∞—

THE CHAIN gate was unhooked and lay limp in the loose dirt of my driveway. A surge of adrenaline spiked through my veins when I saw the Harley leaning on its stand at the foot of my front porch. The Super Glide was spotless, painted the color of black cherries and reflecting the light of the low-hanging sun. I looked toward the sorting corral, but saw no one. The ranch hands had not yet returned.

I drew the Colt out of my holster and crept to the side door, hoping to get some sense of what was happening inside. I poked my head slowly up over the sill, and could only catch a glimpse of my wife, her posture attentive and erect and pressed deep into the cushions of our sofa. She appeared oddly composed, with one hand on the forestock and the other on the trigger of the shotgun that rested on her lap.

I slipped inside as silently as I was able and inched toward the living room, my revolver locked and loaded. I bore my sights down on the bridge of the intruder's nose before I had time to determine who it was.

"Oh good, you're here," Rex Blackwood said.

He was seated opposite Jesse, one leg crossed over the other, perched comfortably in the upholstered lounge chair I favored when watching TV. His attitude and expression were calm and relaxed, but the muscles beneath his eyes and the pulse that showed at his temple told me that he was wound up like a spring trap. It was not the chemical-driven, hair-trigger tension I associated with junkies and armed thieves; it was the full body awareness that was the manifestation of rigorous training.

"Did this man threaten you?" I breathed.

"I'm fine," she said. "He told me that he knows you, but he doesn't look like any friend of yours."

"You'll notice she is the one with the Browning pointed at my throat," Blackwood said to me. He had not once moved his eyes away from Jesse's as he spoke. "For the record, I have no doubt whatsoever that she would pull the trigger if she felt the need to. Any chance you could stop aiming it at me?"

"What in the hell is the matter with you, Blackwood, coming out here unannounced?" I said.

He wore loose-fitting BDU fatigues and a blue-and-white striped shirt, a three-quarter length duster hanging open and unbuttoned over a faded denim vest. His wardrobe struck me as the stylistic opposite of the steel-stud crusted, leather-clad bike thug whose clothing squeaked and jangled from half a block away. Instead Blackwood was outfitted not only for the highway, but for stealth and physical engagement. The only leather he was wearing could be found on the soles of his paratrooper boots.

"Are you heeled, Blackwood?" I asked.

"I exercise my right to keep and bear," he answered, careful that his hands never moved from their positions on the soft arms of my chair.

"Don't leave me guessing," I said.

"There's a .44 pistol in a holster underneath my left arm; a .32-caliber Sauer on my right calf, and a Gerber fighting knife strapped to my left. Would you like me to unpack?"

"No," I said. "But I'd love to hear why you came into my house armed for an insurrection."

"I never face the threat of violence unarmed. And I'm not only referring to your wife."

I reseated the hammer of my Colt and sat down on the couch beside her.

"You can stand down now, Jesse," I said. "Meet Rex Blackwood. He was with me the other night at the Blossom."

She shifted the muzzle six inches to the left, but kept her index finger inside the trigger guard. "That's supposed to make me feel better?"

Dusk had fallen, and I heard Wyatt barking in the distance. I knew that at least part of the crew was returning. I hoped it was not the group that had my daughter riding with them.

"Any reason we couldn't have had this discussion by phone?" I asked.

"I don't trust telephones. This is a face-to-face kind of thing."

The clock on the mantel ticked off several seconds, and the sound of horse hooves was growing nearer.

"Can we cut to it, please?" I asked. "As it turns out, life is short."

Blackwood scratched at the stubble of his beard and shot a glance out the window.

"You've been correct not to underestimate the Charlatans," he said. "I assume you're aware of their history."

I nodded and Blackwood shifted his gaze back indoors, looking first to Jesse, then to me.

"In the late forties they were one of the gangs that overran Hollister, California. Four thousand bikers took over a town and 4,500 of its citizens. Their police force at the time was seven men. They occupied the place for three full days. I don't need to tell you how that went.

"In '69 they were with the Hells Angels at Altamont when the Angels killed Meredith Hunter. The bike clubs had been hired as 'security' for a Stones concert. The promoters paid them with cases of beer."

"I don't—"

"Let me finish," he said. "A few months ago in a small town in the Black Hills, they lit the highway on fire with gasoline and took turns driving through the flames. But not before they shot holes in all the town's fire trucks.

"They make their money dealing weed, speed, and sunshine. Assault and murder are not crimes to them, but rites of fraternal passage. They are dangerous and unpredictable, and they hold no inhibitions about tracking their shit all over your world."

I looked across the couch at Jesse, and saw that her eyes had gone stone cold.

"This is what you came here to tell me?" I asked.

"I came here to ask you a question."

Fingers of light shone through branches of white oak and cedar as the floodlights switched on at the corral down below. The stock horses were being turned out for the night and their sounds floated up with the light.

"Ask it," I said.

"Can you think of a good reason that a Charlatan with a bandaged-up hoof would be visiting with your sheriff at his house?"

My mouth went dry and I felt like I'd swallowed a road flare.

"I couldn't think of one, either," Blackwood said. "I thought you'd like to know. I'll let myself out."

CHAPTER EIGHTEEN

I RESTED MY forearms on the top rail of the fence and watched the stock horses take turns at the trough. A dun gelding rolled on his back in the dirt then kicked to his feet and strolled over to me for a treat, his coat powdered with dust. One by one, I offered him chunks of a carrot I broke off from the flat of my palm. He nuzzled my jacket pocket in search of more, but found none, so he swatted his tail along his flanks and slinked away.

I lit a cigarette and watched the gnats and moths gather in the curtain of luminous heat generated by the floodlight. A colony of brown bats darted along the periphery and disappeared into the dark.

I saw Caleb come out of the office and lock the door behind him. He removed his hat, combed fingers through his gray hair, and walked slowly over to me. His shirt was stained with crescents of dried sweat beneath his arms and trail grit traced the creases of his face.

"We got all the animals put out like you wanted," Caleb said. "And the boys set up a watch schedule for tonight."

"I appreciate that, Caleb," I said. "Did you ever find any family for Dub Naylor?"

"A sister in Big Pine, Montana."

"Can you write down her name and number for me? I'd like to give her a call."

"Already spoke to her. She's driving down to claim the body and take him home."

"How'd she take it?"

"'Bout like you'd expect." Caleb shook his head and shoved his hands into the back pockets of his jeans. "A cowboy oughtta die of old age in a border town whorehouse. Ain't supposed to get shot off his horse herding Purples."

I shook a cigarette out of the pack for him and handed over my lighter.

"They're coming, aren't they?" Caleb asked.

"They're coming."

"When?"

"Soon, I'd guess."

Caleb exhaled through his nose and pushed his hat brim off his forehead. The air was heavy with the smell of apple blossoms and damp earth.

"Got a plan in mind?" he asked.

"Yeah."

"Care to share it with me?"

I got down on my haunches and drew a diagram of the ranch in the dirt between us. When we had finished talking, he took a long last drag, crushed out the butt, and squinted up into the stars.

"Have I mentioned how much I hate your new job?" he said.

———

WE ATE DINNER as a family at the kitchen table for the first time since Cricket had come home. Jesse served the Easter meal she'd prepared for us the day before, but we hadn't had the opportunity to eat.

Wyatt lay on the floor beneath the table, between Cricket and me, waiting for my daughter to feed him table scraps she snuck off of her plate. I caught her in the act and winked, saw an echo of the smile I used to see on her face when she was just a girl, riding her first pony or the time I taught her how to parallel park her car. Jesse had set the table with a pair of pillar candles and a vase she'd filled with anemone and poppies. The flicker of the light reflected in her eyes and I felt the piquant slip of time that was so disconcertingly common to men of my age. I had been harsh in my judgments of my daughter and her friends, and had the sudden realization that it was not that children grow too fast, but that perhaps I had grown too slowly.

My train of thought was interrupted by the ringing of the phone. Jesse shot a glance at me, and the warm light in her dimmed. We had spoken earlier, after Blackwood left, and I laid the whole thing on the table. The facts were ugly and unpleasant, but when the conversation ended I was left with no doubt about her courage or her strength.

I lifted the receiver from the wall phone, dragged the coiled cord behind me, and walked into the living room to talk.

"I'm driving up to Salem in the morning to meet with the BLM," Teresa Pineu told me. "I have you to thank for that."

"You stood your ground, Teresa, you and the kids. Best part is, you did it without anyone getting hurt."

"I don't know if that last statement is true."

"What do you mean by that?"

She drew a breath and fell silent for so long I thought I'd lost her.

"It's the reason I called tonight," she said. "There's a state trooper standing in my house who wants to talk with you.

He won't give me any details except there's been some kind of incident."

"What kind of incident? What's he doing at your place?"

"Something happened not too far from here, out on the state road. He thought it might involve someone who had been camping on my property."

"Who?"

"I don't know, there's just too many of them," she said. "I'm not sure he does either."

"Put him on," I said.

———◦◦◦———

THE BURNED-UP vehicle had been discovered on a gravel turnout along a remote stretch of the state road about twelve miles from the ranch belonging to Teresa Pineu. It had settled on its wheel rims, the tires themselves having long since ruptured and nearly liquefied from the heat of the conflagration that consumed it.

At its apogee the blaze had reached a temperature in excess of 1,700 degrees, enough to cause the roof to sag down like a hammock, melt glass, and crystallize the springs inside the seats. The paint had blistered and blackened over most of the exterior surface, but even so, I had no difficulty identifying it as the piss-yellow van that belonged to the filmmaker Peter Davis and his partner, Sly.

The state trooper I had spoken with on the phone was standing near the rear doors of the van, hands on his hips and speaking with a short, thickset civilian wearing glasses who was busy marking notes on a sheaf of papers fixed to a clipboard. Their profiles cast long shadows on the pebbles, backlit by the headlights of the trooper's patrol car, its Mars Lights coloring their faces with deep red oscillations.

"You must be Dawson," the trooper said. "My name's Wilkens. We spoke on the phone."

He offered me his hand to shake and tucked his thumbs beside the buckle of his utility belt and rocked back on his boots in a way that was meant to maximize his height. His face was youthful and unlined, blond hair cropped close beneath the lemon-squeezer campaign hat tilted forward on his brow.

"This is Dr. Hill, the medical examiner," Wilkens said.

The ME acknowledged me with a nod, without moving his eyes off of his notes.

A pump truck manned by volunteers from the Meridian station was parked on the opposite side of the two-lane, the men milling aimlessly beside it, waiting for some kind of direction from someone in authority.

"Who was first on scene?" I asked.

"I was," Wilkens said. "I saw the glow in the sky from quite a ways away. The vehicle was fully involved by the time I pulled up here. I radioed dispatch and they sent the ME and the fire guys."

"And then you found the time to call me on the phone?"

He squinted past me, toward the firefighters, nostrils flared.

"There was nothing I could do here, Mr. Dawson, so when the ME and my backup arrived I went out to the Pineu ranch where all the hippies had been camped."

"Where's your backup now?"

"He continued his patrol after I returned."

Dr. Hill lowered his clipboard and stepped over between Wilkens and me.

"The protocol is not to disturb a burning vehicle when any victims are obviously beyond medical attention. We don't want to disturb any evidence if it proves to be a crime scene. It's the reason those firefighters aren't hosing down the vehicle."

The air smelled of superheated metal, melted rubber, and petroleum. I circled toward the rear doors and saw for the first time what Dr. Hill had been observing.

"Someone chained all the doors shut."

"Christ," I said. "Is there anyone inside?"

"Take a look for yourself. The rear windows melted out."

I stepped up close and felt the heat radiating from the blackened openings. The interior looked like the inside of an oven that had been left on broil overnight, the sickening odor of scorched steel and electrical wiring and cauterized flesh was one I would always associate with the aftermath of the tank battle at Pyongtaek. On the floor inside lay two incinerated bodies, their limbs drawn up in a pugilistic manner, white patches of bone clearly visible where their scalps and faces had been charred and left their lips drawn back in the rictus of silent screams. Their limbs had grown entangled in the loops and runs of cables and sound booms. The victims' clothing and their bedding and the detritus of their camera equipment had been completely soaked in gasoline; the mineral smell still permeated the night air. Scratch marks on the inside panels showed where Peter and Sly had, in their final futile moments, tried to claw their way out through the metal with their fingernails.

"They were burned alive," the doctor said.

I was familiar with the signs, but did not care to speak. The scratch marks on the interior walls and the soot and ash around their mouths and nasal cavities told me everything I needed to know. I had seen this horror show before, a lifetime ago.

"The clothing acted like a wick," he continued, his tone dispassionate and professorial. "It absorbs the victims' body fat and burns just like a candle."

"Those are human beings," I said.

The ME ignored my remark, bent at the waist, and cocked his head, gazed along the undercarriage, his stomach swelling over the edge of his tooled belt. The stones around the van's perimeter had been blackened, but the gravel underneath appeared untouched.

"I am aware that they are humans," he said, blinking at me behind the lenses of his horn-rimmed glasses. His expression betrayed nothing, only the blank appearance of an obese owl. "An accelerant was used to cause this blaze. The lack of oxygen at the—"

"So, they didn't chain the doors themselves and immolate one another?" I asked. "How did you get through medical school?"

"I was trying to—"

"I don't need to hear it from you. I can smell it for myself."

The ME was craning his neck, splayfooted and gazing past me, into the trees along the roadside.

"Is there a reason you won't look me in the eye when you talk to me?" I said.

Dr. Hill removed his glasses and wiped the lenses with his shirttail. When he was finished, he tucked his shirttail back in place, put his glasses on, and finally looked at me.

"I don't like being stuck between factions," he said.

"What factions are you referring to?"

"Just leave me be, and let me do my work."

"I want to hear you say my name," I said.

"Tyler Dawson."

"Do you know who I am?"

"The new undersheriff."

I shook my head.

"You performed an autopsy on a man who worked for me," I said. "That killing wasn't self-inflicted, either, by the way. You never had the decency to follow up with me. That man had a family too. Just like the two young men inside that van."

"I told you everything I could," he said. "The investigation is out of my hands, unless I'm called to testify. I gave the sheriff and the DA everything I had just like they asked. I'm not lying."

"The level of your veracity is no concern of mine. You're the one who's got to look at yourself shaving every morning."

"I am sorry about your cowboy."

"You are a walking feed sack," I said. "My cowboy had a name. But I don't want to hear it on your lips."

His mouth moved like a fish left on the planking of a pier as I turned my attention to the trooper.

"This doesn't look like the work of the Charlatans to you, Wilkens? You are aware of the hippie protestors at Pineu's— enough so that you drove all the way out there just to call me—but the presence of an armed gang of California bikers doesn't register with you? Have you bothered to put out a bulletin on your radio?"

"I don't need you to—"

"Shut up and write down the names of these two victims: one is Peter Davis; the other one's first name is Sylvester. I do not know his last. Stop staring at me."

"I phoned you because it is protocol," Wilkens said. The tendons on his neck stood out like steel cords.

"You phoned me because someone told you to," I said. "Do you think it's a coincidence that the two men in that van were tortured to death by the Charlatans and their cameras and film stock destroyed? They were shooting a documentary about everything that's been happening up here."

The gravel under my boots was dotted with balls of shattered windshield glass that glittered in the blinking lights of the patrol car.

"Where do you think you're going?" Wilkens asked.

"I'm leaving you to your crime scene."

"It's your county, Dawson. This scene belongs to you."

"It appears to me that it's Lloyd Skadden's county," I said. "And the state road is your jurisdiction."

My eyes fell on the departmental logo painted on the open door of his cruiser.

"You've done your job, Trooper. You dragged me all the way out here for nothing. You can tell whoever it is who pulls your levers that they got my attention, and the next time they see me I'll be flying a black flag."

"I don't know what you're talking about."

I recalled the government vehicles that had so rapidly departed Teresa Pineu's ranch on Easter Sunday.

"You make a poor liar," I said.

He stepped in close to me then, so close our hat brims nearly touched.

"Would you care to repeat that remark?"

"What would be the purpose?" I said. "You heard me fine the first time."

I climbed into the cab of my truck and slammed the door, and the glowing eyes of a roving herd of deer stared back at me from deep inside the trees. I switched on the Motorola that we'd found at the Meridian substation, waited for the ready light, and thumbed the mic.

"Caleb, this is Dawson."

Nothing answered me but silence, so I tried a second time and my pulse began to quicken. Another long moment passed with no reply. Far to the north along the edges of the mountain range a cloud lit up with lightning and I heard the static crack inside the speaker of my radio. The damned thing was useless, impeded either by the weather or the distance or the mountainous terrain. My tires spun in the loose stones as I floored the accelerator and fishtailed out onto the asphalt.

The wind had begun to quicken. I could see it in the tops of the trees as I drove, their limbs whipping broadly against the black sky. Small branches had already snapped off from the cedars and I felt the truck fame jolt and shudder when I failed to maneuver around one of them. Fine beads of sweat ran down my back and I felt my shirt stick to my skin.

Seven miles up, I pulled off the road at the first phone booth I could find. It stood adjacent to a Texaco gas station and a tire repair shop whose windows reflected dull blue neon light. I dropped a dime into the slot and dialed Caleb, stared through the graffiti-scarred plexiglass and up into the star-splattered sky while I impatiently counted out the ringtones.

"Wheeler," he said after the fifth one.

"Tell Jesse it's time," I said. "Tell everybody to get ready."

"Say that again," Caleb said.

"It's happening tonight."

CHAPTER NINETEEN

ALL THE LIGHTS around the Diamond D had been extinguished by the time I arrived back home. I drove in through the dirt service road that traced a shallow arc from the two-lane to the barn through several acres of heavily wooded native timber. I turned off my headlights and drove cautiously by memory and the meager light that shone down from a half moon that floated behind a veil of rapidly moving clouds.

I cut the engine and shifted into neutral, allowing gravity to let me coast the last hundred yards in silence, and pulled to a stop behind a stand of shrubs. I jumped out of the truck and blazed a trail through the overgrowth of timothy and June grass, stopping every few yards to squat down on my haunches and strain my ears inside the weeds. It took me several minutes to reach the outskirts of the ranch, where I hunkered down surrounded by a thicket of wildwood just short of the main house. I allowed my eyes to adjust more fully to the darkness and saw a string of gray smoke from the fireplace burning in the living room stitch a broken line between the chimney and the sky. The air was heavy with woodsmoke and ozone and the smell of rainfall and crushed grass.

I had no way of knowing where, or if, any intruders had entered before me, but the outright absence of night noise set off alarm bells in my head. No insects chirred inside the brush, nor frogs making noise from the creek on the far side of the barn. The only sounds came from the sigh of the wind and the creaking from the limbs of conifers high overhead.

As a young boy my father had told me a story about how my grandfather had acquired the Diamond D ranch. In that parable, my grandfather encountered a man listlessly pulling at the soil with a hoe beside a dugout he had carved into an esker. He asked the man how he had come to possess the property, and the man replied, "I fought for it." A moment went by, and another, as my grandfather considered his options. After a while he said to the man, "Then, how about I fight *you* for it."

The story affected me strangely back then, sometimes filling me with a sense of unease so profound that I felt I may never be worthy to hold title to something for which someone else's blood might have been shed. Squatting there in the dark I had no time to reflect on abstractions, but the full measure of the parable's meaning had suddenly settled in on me.

I caught a movement in my peripheral vision, little more than a shadow that crept across the darkness. The form moved quickly past the side of the barn and disappeared again as it rounded the corner to the rear. A bright and sudden flash of light sliced into my field of vision, and I had an instant confirmation as to what was going on.

My experience with gangs, as with bullies of any stripe, was that they ascribed little value to advance strategy. Instead they relied almost exclusively on the full-frontal blitz of unexpected assault and on the chaos and the terror it is meant to inspire in its victims. I had laid down my chips on that conviction, and had wagered my own life and those belonging to my family and my friends on its legitimacy.

The detonation of the points of fire ignited in rapid succession, explosions made by flaming bottles filled with gasoline being shattered against the slat walls of my barn. Though I had no prior knowledge as to what their specific methods might entail, I believed that the attackers' first maneuver would be to create a diversion intended to lure me outside and leave Jesse and Cricket exposed and alone inside the house.

I sprinted toward the barn, in the direction of the last of the explosions, arriving just as the bomber attempted his escape through the barn door, and slammed my shoulder deep into his sternum. We hit the ground together, and I rolled him on his back and straddled him, landing a swift kite to the hollow of his throat as he struggled to throw me off. He clawed and grasped and finally wrapped his hand around the fighting knife sheathed on his belt, and I leaped off as it sliced the air where my face had been only a fraction of a second before.

Inside the barn, I could see the flames licking at the horse stall doors and climbing up the walls toward the hay bales. He moved in on me, slashing his blade through the air in-between us, and I backed myself toward the burning structure.

I snatched a lariat from the hook inside the door and scythed it before me in defense. I slid my hands along the braiding until I located the knot beneath my fingers, never taking my eyes from the flicker of fire reflected on the planes of his face as he continued to angle in on me. In one unexpected motion, I slid backward, dug my bootheels deep into the dirt, and threw a heel-rope loop toward his feet. It noosed up tight around his ankles and I tipped him to the ground like deadfall. He landed hard and broke the grip on the handle of his blade and I dragged him facedown across the ground.

He squirmed and reached down to his ankles to loosen the knot that bound him, but I landed a swift kick to the base of his skull that stilled him with the swiftness of a bolt gun. His head lolled forward. He was semiconscious, but I knew he'd come back around.

I used the short time advantage I had gained to wrap the rope around his shins and run a line up to his wrists, then I dragged him all the way inside the burning barn. I pulled the loose end of pulley chain and strung the hook between the bindings on his ankles, raised him up and tied him off to a steel cleat bolted into the wall, and hung him upside down like a moth cocoon, about five feet off the ground.

Hot smoke roiled inside the space and burned my eyes while I forked a stack of sawdust and dry straw underneath the dangling biker and watched him start to squirm and twist as he began to regain consciousness. I topped off the straw pile with an old inner tube from a hay barrow, an old and ugly trick I'd learned that intensifies the heat and duration of an open flame.

"What the fuck?" he said, and fought against his bindings.

"You've developed a dangerous fixation with fire, Wallace," I said.

The taste of smoke seared my throat as I collected my breath, and I watched a trickle of blood that had collected in his hair seep out and trace a narrow line along his forehead.

"The boys are going to take turns skull fucking your old lady and your daughter, and they're gonna make you watch."

"That is an ugly way to speak about my family."

"You're not going to let me burn to death."

"The smoke'll probably kill you first," I said.

He blinked away the tears that had gathered in his eyes from heat and smoke and squinted at me as the first trickle of his own blood dripped to the floor.

"How many men are with you?" I asked.

"Go fuck yourself."

"See you later, Wallace."

"You're not going to leave me here."

"Look in my eyes and tell me if you think I'm lying."

I pulled a handkerchief from the back pocket of my jeans and rolled it into a tube. He shook his head violently as I tried to gag him, so I quieted him down with a swift right jab that cracked the bridge of his nose and sounded like a snapping twig. He choked and spat as his own fresh blood flowed freely into his mouth and gathered in his throat.

"They're going to kill you, motherfucker," he coughed.

"Says the man strung up inside my hayloft like a hog."

I patted him on the back as I stepped toward the door.

"Six," he called out.

"Six men," I said. "Including you?"

"Let me down."

"Talk to me, Wallace."

"Yes, goddamn it," he said. "Six including me."

"You and five other men come to my ranch to assault my family and I should haul you down?"

I wrestled the handkerchief between his teeth and tied it tight at the back of his head.

"You're going to burn, Wallace, like the boys you torched inside their van. I wish I could stick around to hear you suffer."

I don't know if he believed that I was bluffing or was counting on my mercy. The expression on his face was one of raw defiance until it disappeared in a single fleeting moment of epiphany as I turned to walk away.

"It will not be easy going for you as you make your way into the next world," I said. "Goodnight, Wallace."

I stepped out into the cool air as white billows from my flaming barn whirled skyward on the wind. A windmill at the edge of the breed-bull corral groaned and shivered as the wheel spun, and I rubbed my eyes with my bruised knuckles as the barn fire reflected in the sheet-metal blades of the fan.

I glanced toward the main house, but it remained cloaked in darkness except for the thin ribbon of smoke that still wafted from the chimney. But a separate blaze had now erupted and backlit the maples next to the office.

I ran to the structure where Caleb had stationed himself, and now saw that the fire I'd seen before was actually coming from twin blazes that had been set behind the storage room and the farrier's shed. I took hold of the windowsill and raised my eyes up over the ledge to look inside the office. Caleb had the barrel of a carbine aimed squarely into the chest of a Charlatan he had wedged into a corner of the room. The biker's lips were moving, but I couldn't make out the words. I pressed my face up to the glass, shielded my eyes from the glare and scanned the recesses, and confirmed that they were alone inside. I crouched down low and moved to the door, pounded three times with the ball of my fist, my signal to Caleb that it was me about to enter.

"There's six of them altogether," I said.

"Figures," Caleb said. "The weak always travel in packs."

"We got any rope in here?"

Caleb nodded toward the broom closet and watched as I bound the Charlatan's hands. He wore the same insolent expression Wallace had, but this one's teeth had been snapped off at the gum line, and the overall effect was that of an imbecilic character in a medieval troupe.

"You know who this one is?" I asked Caleb.

"Couldn't care less."

"This one likes to sodomize young girls and burn their skin with cigarette butts."

"Emily Meeghan?" he asked.

I nodded.

"Do you know much about breeding cattle?" I said to the rapist.

"Kiss my ass," he lisped.

"I used to have three breeding bulls," I told him. "But one of them exploded. Still trying to figure that out. Thing is, it leaves the other two bulls with a lot of extra work to do, so we need to keep them pretty revved up. You know what I'm talking about, right?"

I went back to the closet and returned carrying a plastic spray bottle. I shook the yellowish contents of the bottle before his eyes, and misted the air with a squeeze of the trigger.

"Smells, don't it?" Caleb said, and turned his head away.

"Tell the rapist here what's in this bottle," I said. "I think he'd appreciate it more than most."

My foreman shot me a look out of the corner of his eye, and I nodded that I meant what I had said.

"What we do to keep things moving in the breed pen is to spray pheromones on the cows," Caleb said. "Now, bulls are goddamned mean to start with, but you give them a whiff of this shit, and Katie-bar-the-door. I mean it's like a dozen drunken sailors on shore leave in Bangkok."

The biker's eyes bugged wild when I began to squirt him down from head to foot.

"You think the two of us can lift this idiot's fat ass?" I asked Caleb.

I wound a length of duct tape around his ankles and we carried him through the door between us like a hammock, in the same way we would when branding a new calf. We hefted his body across the top rail of the breeding corral and I slit the tape binding his feet. The bull snorted and blew when he got his first whiff of the juice. Even in the dark, I could make out the whites of the animal's wild eyes as he trotted over from the far side of the arena.

"I'm going to leave your hands tied, to make it fair for the bull," I said. "Just like you did for Emily."

The biker made a mewling sound as Caleb and I shoved him the rest of the way over the fence. I could feel the pounding of the bull's hooves as he broke into a run.

"He's either gonna stomp you or fuck you to death," Caleb said. "Either way, it sounds like something you're familiar with."

———

WE CAUGHT the tail end of a message coming through the speakers of the handheld radio unit on Caleb's desk as we came in. Caleb thumbed the transmit button and requested a repeat. The radios hadn't been worth a damn for me out on the highway, but at least they functioned here on the ranch.

"I've got one injured in the shed," Taj Caldwell said. "He's leaking pretty good."

"I'm going to the house," I told Caleb.

"Alone?"

"Powell and Griffin are supposed to be in there," I said. "You give Taj some backup and meet me in the house when you get his situation buttoned up."

Caleb picked up the transmitter and I thought of something else.

"Tell Taj to try to get the barn fire under control. Take the pump and hoses to the cistern—"

"I know how to fight a goddamned fire," Caleb said.

His manner changed when he read the expression on my face.

"You're going to find one of them in the barn," I said.

"Is he dead?"

"I don't know, maybe," I said. "Either way, I want you to leave him where you find him, exactly where he is. Let the medical examiner haul him down."

"Haul him down from where?"

"You'll see," I said. "You gonna be okay, Caleb?"

"Don't say shit like that to me. I may be old, but I can keep my ass in the saddle same as you."

I hadn't taken three steps outside before I heard a fusillade of shots echo down to me from the inside of my house. I fought the urge to run straight in, but knew it could turn into an ambush. Instead, I drew my Colt, crept up the slope between the trees, and circled toward the rear entrance of the house.

To the north, the clouds and lightning I had seen before were growing in intensity. Some time tomorrow, the rain that they turned loose over the mountains would flow down into the valley, swelling creeks and rivers with brown water, mud, and driftwood. Overhead I felt the spectral presence of those bats again, careening in the dark.

No lights burned inside the house as I cut wide around the far corner of the garden, underneath the willow with the chimes that hung inside, only a yellow glow that lit the windowpanes from flames that licked the logs inside the fireplace. One saddled horse grazed riderless and alone beside the fruit orchard, dragging its reins along the soil, too dark for me to see whose mount it was.

The mudroom door was already ajar when I approached it, so I eased it back on its hinges as silently as I could and slipped inside. A man lay dead, seated on the floor, his back resting against the cabinets. A bullet had cored his forehead and removed the back side of his skull and the contents of his brainpan streaked across the panels.

I stepped over the dead man's outstretched legs and crossed the threshold into the kitchen. I heard a tapping sound at the far end of the room, somewhere deep inside the shadows. I crabbed sideways keeping the counter at my back, my eyes and pistol aimed inward toward a gap in the wall that opened onto the living room. The tapping grew louder, more insistent, and I saw the supine shape of another man pressed into the far corner of the kitchen.

I recognized the boots and moved more swiftly toward him. Griffin lay in the dark, a puncture wound high up on his chest and a bullet hole pulsing dun-colored blood from his thigh. Moonlight from the window shone down on his face, shiny with perspiration and the color of a spent coal brick. His lips were drawn into a tight cone of pain, but his eyes were burnished with light. He was tapping on the wall with trembling fingers and spoke to me in a whisper.

"There's two dead in there," he said, casting a glance in the direction of the living room.

"Cricket and Jesse?"

He shook his head slowly and his lips made a dry smacking sound as he tried to speak.

It dawned on me I hadn't heard the dog bark.

"And Wyatt?"

"Somebody kicked the hell out of that dog," he managed. "Powell took 'em all down to the root cellar."

I grabbed the damp dish towels from the counter and pressed one into the pulsing hole in his leg. He grimaced and sucked in his breath while I stuffed the cloth inside and strapped it in place with another. His shirt had soaked up the leakage from the wound near his shoulder, and the blood did not appear to be spreading. I knelt down beside Griffin, and leaned in close to hear him.

"I'm sorry," he rasped. "We were late. Some of them were already inside."

I squeezed his good shoulder to tell him it was okay, and urged him to continue speaking if he was able. He told me that Powell and he had helped Paul Tucker set the wire, but it had taken longer than they'd expected. By the time they finally arrived at the house, two bikers were already inside. One had taken hold of Cricket, an arm locked around her waist and attempting to drag her to the floor. The other was coming for Jesse, but she caught him on the side of his jaw with a fierce swing of a fire iron that knocked him face-first into the box. Cricket slipped loose and picked up the iron Jesse had dropped and swung down on the back of the injured man's head.

"She wouldn't stop," Griffin told me. "It sounded like a rotted pumpkin being crushed by a ball bat."

The second one leapt over the back of the couch and grabbed hold of Cricket again. Jesse snatched up the carbine she'd tucked in the corner next to the sideboard and went after the one that had a hand on Cricket. Wyatt went after him and caught his pant leg in his teeth. The biker kicked him viciously and the dog slid, half-unconscious, across the hardwood floor.

"That's when Powell and me come in, Mr. Dawson. Jesse had the man backed up against the wall, but he still had hold of your daughter's wrist. Jesse cut loose with that rifle I don't know how many times, and dropped that man straight to the floor."

I cocked back the hammer on the Colt and held it up at a ninety-degree angle. I found myself in the living room, and it was just as Griffin had described. Several shots had stitched holes in the wall paneling and stuffing spilled out from rents carved deep into the pads on the sofa. Shell casings littered the floor.

A denim-clad body lay half in and half out of the fireplace and the room stank of singed clothing and charred meat and hair. The back of the biker's head looked like a crushed pomegranate and the case-hardened fire tool lay on the floor beside him, bent at an unnatural angle.

I shifted around the edge of a table and saw the other man slumped at the base of the wall. His eyes were still wide open, as though he had been caught completely unaware. His zipper and the buckle of his belt had been unfastened and the loose end hung down between his thighs like a lascivious tongue.

A pink halo of gristle and white chunks of flesh stained the wall where one of the blasts had taken him straight through the lungs. A red spume of pulmonary blood still frothed on his lips and seeped into the dark tangled mass of his beard. One perfect hole spidered out from a stray shot that had passed through the bay window and stared back at me like the all-seeing eye of a mute witness.

I returned to the kitchen, picked up the phone, and dialed the emergency room at County General. I told them to send as many ambulances and medical personnel as they had on hand, then hung up and knelt down next to Griffin again.

"You doing okay, Sam?"

He nodded his head and the lids of his eyes began to flutter. I slapped his face gently with the pad of my hand and told him to keep his eyes open.

"Old Caleb is coming any minute now," I told him. "I'll stay right here with you 'til he does."

Griffin nodded but said nothing.

"Are you aware of the significance of your name?" I asked, but didn't wait for an answer. I just wanted to keep him awake. "The mythology of the griffin goes back centuries before Christ. Half eagle and half lion, he denotes strength and military courage. Griffins were the guardians and protectors of a kingdom's most priceless treasures. You knew all that, right, Samuel?"

"No, sir," Griffin whispered, and the corners of his mouth curved into a smile. "I didn't."

"I'd say you lived up to the name," I told him. "You protected the two people most precious to me."

"One of the men got away," Griffin said.

"He won't get far," I said.

Caleb pushed in through the front door. I heard his footfalls on the wood floor as he stopped there, taking in the carnage spread across the living room.

"In the kitchen, Caleb," I called out. "It's all clear in here."

He stopped in his tracks and inhaled deeply when his eyes first fell on Griffin lying there beside me in a viscous pool of his own blood. Caleb placed his Winchester on the table and tipped his hat back off his forehead with his fist.

"Ambulances should be on the way," I said. "Keep pressure on the wound on Sam's leg, and make sure he stays conscious."

Caleb nodded and began to speak, but I cut him off.

"Jesse and Cricket are in the cellar with Powell. They're safer in there than up here, at least until help arrives."

Caleb glared at me, his expression blank.

"Where in the hell do you think you're going?" he said.

CHAPTER TWENTY

PART OF THE barn's roof had caved in on itself and collapsed in a shower of orange embers. A vast cloud of steam and smoke rose into the sky behind me as I made my way back to the truck, and I knew Taj had begun hosing down the fires. A freight train sounded its pneumatic horn somewhere far up the valley and the sound echoed from between the walls of stone canyons and creek beds, propelled by the wind inside the storm. I could almost hear the grind of the steel wheels along the hot flanges of track as the train prepared for the steep climb up the grade.

My headlights glanced off the rough surface of the corduroy road and I rolled down my window as the beams lighted the scene where the runaway biker had met up with my wrangler, Paul Tucker.

Both of the entry roads into the ranch had been strung with loops of razor wire that had been placed in the low spots between rises, where runoff had carved natural gullies, knowing anyone unfamiliar with the place would not see the hazard until there was nothing they could do to avoid it. The original intent had been to keep the bastards out, but the call I had made to Caleb from the phone booth had obviously come too late for that. Even so, I knew it would be useful as a deterrent to an escape.

"That's gotta hurt," I said.

Tucker grinned and laid the barrel of his rifle across his right shoulder. His eyes shone inside the lean angles of his face, reflecting the glare of my headlamps.

"He come barreling down that road like a bat out of hell," Tucker told me. "Never saw it comin' until it was too late. Sumbitch's brakes wouldn't grab on the loose dirt and he laid down that hog and slid straight into the coils."

"Looks like he's tangled up good."

"I told him to stop fightin', it just makes it worse."

"Doesn't look like he took your advice."

Tucker turned and spit a stream of tobacco juice into the weeds, wiped his lips with the sleeve of his jacket.

"Naw," he said. "He's a foul-mouthed sumbitch—stubborn too. What do you want me to do with him?"

"Leave him be. If he gets loose somehow, shoot him in the leg," I told him. "If that doesn't stop him, shoot him in the other leg."

The corners of his eyes twitched, not with surprise but anticipation.

"You joshin' me, Mr. Dawson?"

"I'm dead serious. There's ambulances coming. But if this piece of shit gives you one lick of trouble, you put him down on the ground."

"Yes, sir," Tucker said and spat again.

"You think I can get this truck around the edge over there? I need to get out to the two-lane."

"I'll guide you through. Follow me, just go slow. It's slippery down there in the low spot."

—⟋⟍⟋—

SEVEN.

I don't know why it angered me so much to know that Wallace had lied to me. I counted again in my head. There had been seven of the bastards on my ranch. I was glad all over again that I'd left him strung up in the barn, and put it out of my head that some moral switch might have been permanently shut down inside me.

I did not hold to an image of a vengeful or vindictive God, nor to the notion that His will held much sway with the improbable and grotesque mischief of venal and prehensile men. I wanted to deny, also, that their acts had been choreographed and were operating with the sanction of an organized society. But I had been made complicit in some scheme of which I had no prior knowledge nor had been given the opportunity to consent. If some arbitrary wheel was being turned, I would not allow me or my family to be strapped to it while it was being set to the torch.

To the extent that I held to a code that I lived by, it had not included violence as a component tool, at least not since I'd come home from Korea. That code had now been revised in the extreme, and I felt no guilt or remorse for my actions, or the ones I may yet have the need to commit.

These were the thoughts that accompanied me as I sped down the road to Lloyd Skadden's ranch.

———⌇⌇⌇———

FAT DROPS of rain exploded on the windscreen of my truck, one drop at a time, desultory and hesitant, and lightning forked high in the clouds.

I parked my truck at an angle, intentionally blocking the exit for a marked patrol car and a dark-colored Harley shovelhead outfitted with ape hangers and a sissy bar. I placed my palm on the cruiser's hood and it felt warm to the touch, as did the carburetor on the hog.

Two uniformed officers and one biker had been shot dead on the stone steps at Lloyd Skadden's front door, the apparent victims of a brief and close range firefight. Lights that had been constructed to resemble gas lamps flickered and cast jittering shadows across the bodies and the troweled swirls of an ornately plastered wall.

I withdrew the Colt strapped to my belt and stepped between the pools of blood that had already begun to congeal onto the stones and mortar. The front door was cracked open, so I cocked the hammer and pushed it slowly open with my shoulder and slid inside. The interior was dim, the only light a golden glow that emanated from an open doorway at the terminus of a short hall at the far side of the sitting room. I had my finger looped around the trigger, ready to let fly, but saw no movement anywhere.

I angled past a mirror at the entry and toward the source of the light, and heard the murmur of male voices coming from inside. Pressing my back against the wall, I crabbed sideways toward the sound, my footsteps muffled by the carpeting. When I peered around the casing, I found myself staring into the twin barrels of a cut-down Remington that I had seen before.

The biker I called Rabbit had his right hand wrapped around the shortened stock. In his left he held a semiautomatic pistol, which was aimed at the side of Lloyd Skadden's head.

"Lower the hammer on your weapon, Mr. Dawson," Rabbit said. "Do it slowly, then remove the cartridges and drop them on the floor. When you're finished, put the gun on the table by the door."

He was perched at the edge of Skadden's desk, his weight resting on his good foot, while the bandaged one swung loosely in the air. His eyes were dry, the pupils spun down to pinpoints with painkillers and speed. He moistened his uneven teeth inside a crooked smile and waited while I thumbed the cylinder release and dropped the unspent shells onto the carpet.

"You come out here alone?" he asked. "Or did you bring your nigger with you?"

"Use that word again and I'll find a way to slit your throat and pull your tongue out through the hole."

"You still mad about that girl at the motel?" he asked. "I thought a worldly man like you would understand a little milking through the fence. You need to learn to lighten up, man. In fact, why don't you take a load off your feet?"

"I'm good where I am."

"Then stand there in the doorway where I can keep an eye on you."

Beneath his Charlatans club vest, he had the sleeves of a flannel shirt rolled up above his forearms. The right one was disfigured by a sheet of purple scar tissue that looked like snake skin or wax paper that had been melted on his flesh.

"Willy Peter," he said when he saw the focus of my gaze. "A keepsake from the war that is not a war."

He tilted his head sideways and took on an expression of amusement.

"I assume you know all about these things," he said. "You've had some experience with armored tanks, if I'm not mistaken."

"How would you know that?"

"Everyone in this town has a big mouth. But that tidbit I learned from this one." He jogged the pistol in his left hand in the direction of Lloyd Skadden.

The back of Skadden's khaki uniform shirt had been soaked through by a line of sweat that traced the humps along his spine. His hands quaked with a combination of fear and helplessness and anger as he knelt and stacked banded bricks of currency into a pair of saddlebags that rested beside the open door of a Hamilton safe that was bolted to the floor.

"We had a spirited disagreement regarding compensation," Rabbit said. "And the sheriff doubted the sincerity of my first request to open up his safe."

His eyes shifted to the corner of Skadden's office, where the sheriff's son, Myron, was still seated in a guest chair, his hands clenched in a death grip on its leather-upholstered arms. One eye was sprung open in surprise; a wet and blackened hole stared out from where the other should have been. His mouth was gaping like a hatchling.

I returned my attention to the Rabbit, who simply looked at me and shrugged.

"I don't care to repeat myself," he said. "There's no negotiation on that point."

"I didn't ask for an explanation."

"I know. I'm just making conversation while we wait."

He leaned toward Lloyd Skadden.

"Speed it up, fat ass," he said out of the side of his mouth. "Has he always been like this?" he said to me. "I can see it on your face. You're wondering why I don't just shoot you where you stand."

I had no interest in provoking a man whose brain was roiling with spiders and had the means to end both Skadden and me within a half second of each other, so I said nothing.

"I'm told that in the old days, Comanche raiders would often let one person live, just to tell the story of the horrors and as a warning to others."

Skadden had finished loading the bags and stood to hand it to the biker.

"Shut and lock the door on that safe and sit down in your chair, fat man," Rabbit said and hooked the bags onto the arm that held the pistol. "Lay that strap across my shoulder before you do."

The sheriff did as he was told and Rabbit stood up from his perch. The bandage on the foot I'd shot was crusted brown with dried bloodstains.

"Sorry you made this personal, Dawson," Rabbit said. "Under different circumstances and all that . . ."

"I doubt it."

"You're right. Probably not. Anyway, I gotta split."

He turned and fired twice, one went low into Skadden's belly and the other grazed his throat. He never took the shotgun's aim off of me.

Rabbit scrunched his face into a grimace as the smell of cordite filled the room.

"Oooh," he said. "That can't feel good."

My eyes were locked on Rabbit's while Skadden slumped down in his chair, hands groping at the new hole in his abdomen. Blood seeped through his fingers and his eyes rolled back into his head.

"Step into the office, Dawson. I'm sure you'll want to help your buddy while I leave."

He saw the calculation I was making in my head.

"You could probably try to get those shells back into your gun and shoot me," he said. He picked up my Colt off the table with his thumb and index finger and tossed it down the hall into the darkness of the living room. "But you'll have to find it first."

Rabbit hobbled backward down the hall and kept me covered with the sawed-off. When he disappeared around the corner, I made my choice and went to see if there was anything I could do for Skadden.

One shot had torn his clavicle to splinters, and had to hurt like hell. But the gut shot was a bad one, and aside from attempting to stanch the bleeding there was little I could do.

I picked up the phone on Skadden's desk, and considered calling the state police, but had no idea who I could trust there anymore; the emergency medical teams were likely still out at my ranch. I decided to call Melissa Vernon of the BLM instead and asked for assistance from anyone she might know with the ODOJ.

Her office would be closed at this hour, so I dialed 411 and got her residential number. Skadden's complexion was going gray and his breathing grew shallower with every second that I waited on the line.

She agreed to have a special investigations unit of the Oregon State Department of Justice sent down to sort this out. I had no way of knowing if I could trust those people either, but it would circumvent the state police and leave the feds out of it too.

"You've used up all your chips with me, Mr. Dawson."

"I'm sorry that you feel that way. I'd appreciate it if you'd send a team down here anyway. It's a mess. I'll wait."

Skadden looked into my face, his expression revealing nothing but confusion and contempt, a man whose certain world had imploded right before his eyes, but could not comprehend how it went so badly wrong.

I tried to speak to him, at the very least to learn the name of the man who was his killer, but he would only stare at me with hatred burning in his eyes.

Lloyd Skadden died ten minutes later, his white and purple viscera bulging out between his knuckles, having never said another word.

—⁘—

LUCIFER WINKED in the predawn sky, bright and sharp beside the waning gibbous moon. In the hours while I awaited the arrival of my backup, I examined the crime scene for myself, made coffee in the kitchen, and phoned Jesse at the ranch.

"Everybody's fine," she said. "When are you coming home?" Her voice betrayed the exhaustion and the shock that followed on from the experience of unbridled terror.

"As soon as I can," I said. "I promise. Some agents from ODOJ will be arriving there, probably before I do. Don't speak to anyone until I get home."

"What am I supposed to do?"

"Give 'em coffee on the gallery and tell them to wait until I come back."

She told me that Sam Griffin had been taken with the others up to County Hospital, and was probably in surgery as we spoke.

"I'm worried about Cricket, Ty."

I felt my heart jump in my chest.

"Sam told me Cricket was okay."

"She is," Jesse said. "That's the problem. She acts like nothing happened here at all."

I took a mug of coffee out to the front of Skadden's house. I sat down on the basin of the Spanish fountain, scanned the surreality of the scene that lay before me in the driveway and lit a cigarette. Somewhere in the bushes a landscape timer clicked and the pump inside the fountain cycled on. The stone bowls overflowed and the incongruous soothing sound of falling water filled the atmosphere and rebounded off the walls. The air was cold and smelled like rain, but the storm I'd seen in last night's sky remained immobile over the mountain peaks.

Dual shafts of yellow headlights slashed through the dark along the entry lined with cypress, and I stood up as three matching black Dodge Coronets pulled inside the gates and parked. Two agents emerged from each of the cars, and looked so oddly similar that they could have dropped off of the edge of some eastern seaboard factory conveyor, been given haircuts and gray suits, and handed leather satchels, cameras, and clipboards.

One man stepped out from the driver's side of the lead car and headed straight for me. He introduced himself as Averill Conrad, lead investigator for the Oregon DOJ. The other five donned rubber gloves and immediately set about snapping photos of the scene and making diagrams and notes.

Averill Conrad removed his Madison hat and ran a hand across a head that had gone prematurely bald. He was short and wiry in stature, so I had a good view of a pate flecked with patches of dry skin and a horseshoe fringe of hair that was the color of a rusted nail. His eyes possessed the peculiar greenish cast of the sky when it presages a monsoon.

"Tyler Dawson," I said, and offered my hand for him to shake. He seemed to consider the alternatives before he took it.

"I don't like dealing with amateurs," he said.

"Are you this agitated every morning when you get up, or is this one something special."

"I don't know you, Dawson."

"Were you ever in the livestock trade? If not, there's not much reason that you would."

"I was told you are the undersheriff in this county."

"Undersheriff is a position I was shanghaied into. Let's get this over with, I need to get back home."

Conrad's naturally ruddy complexion reddened further and he kept his eyes locked onto mine while he screwed his hat back into place. His blunt and squared-off features put me in mind of a poorly tempered Dexter bull, and I could not take my eyes off of a patch just off the center of his chin that he had missed with his razor that morning.

I walked him through the scene and gave him my statement. I identified Skadden's two dead deputies by name as we passed by them on our way into the house. We ended up in Skadden's office and stood on opposite sides of the desk.

"So, this rabbit-faced biker shot Sheriff Skadden for no reason?"

"I suspect his reason was to keep me occupied while he made his escape," I said.

"And he left you alive."

"He said something about Comanches leaving one live witness as a warning."

"What the hell is that supposed to mean?"

"I guess you'll have to ask him when you find him."

My focus drifted to the safe that was bolted to Skadden's floor. The door was closed and locked, and I still was not convinced that I trusted Averill Conrad, so I kept any mention of money to myself.

Special Investigator Conrad and I went through the entire scene two more times, and I repeated my recitation of events nearly verbatim. I had grown tired of this guy's condescending attitude, and it was long past time for me to get back to my ranch. I lit a cigarette and moved toward the door.

"I would prefer it if you wouldn't smoke," Conrad said.

"So would my wife, but you can see how that worked out."

He cut his eyes out through the door, squinted at the sky that had faded pale blue with the rising sun.

"We're not finished here," he said.

"I am."

"The entire cadre of Meriwether County law enforcement is lying dead on this property, and you tell me you're leaving?"

"You need to adjust your thinking, Conrad. The *surviving* members of this county's law enforcement cadre are either lying in a hospital bed or waiting for me at the crime scene that I used to refer to as my house."

"This is the reason I don't like dealing with amateur law enforcement."

"Tell you the truth, Conrad, I'm not overly impressed with the qualities I've seen among the so-called professionals in these parts either. Let's call it a draw."

I could feel his eyes peeling the skin off the back of my neck as I walked over to my truck and opened the door.

"We're colleagues, Mr. Conrad," I said. "Whether you like that or not. I've answered all your questions and now I'm heading home. When you have something else for me, you know where to find me."

"I'll be in touch," he called out to me.

"You'd better be," I said. "This thing's a long damn way from over."

CHAPTER TWENTY-ONE

JESSE AND CRICKET met me on the porch when I got home. Four men identical to those I had left behind at Lloyd Skadden's house were now going through similar machinations inside of mine. Flash bulbs ignited from the other side of the window and left their floating shadows imprinted on my eyes.

"They just barged in and started up with that," Jesse said. "I offered coffee like you said, but they refused."

I hugged my wife and daughter close, and breathed them in. I could feel Jesse begin to falter.

"I was only halfway kidding when I said that on the phone," I told her. "You didn't speak to them yet, did you?"

"No," Cricket said, the expression on her face unreadable to me. "We told them we weren't willing to speak to them until you got here."

"I told Caleb and the others what you said," Jesse said as she moved out of my arms. "No one's given any statements."

I moved down the stairs and looked in the direction of the barn. It had burned to the foundations, its previous existence marked by a mound of blackened beams, charred timber, and smoldering ash. From where I stood, I could see Taj Caldwell spraying water from the hose and pump that snaked out from the cistern onto the glowing coals that steamed inside the wreckage. Caleb drove the tractor, scooping piles of wet ash and debris into the dump truck that we used for hauling rubbish to the transfer station. Tucker sat behind the wheel and tossed a wave in my direction.

"Are you Tyler Dawson?" one of the gray suits called down from the porch behind me.

"I'm Dawson."

"I need to speak with you now, sir."

"In a minute," I said and headed down to talk with Caleb Wheeler first.

He kept the tractor running while he climbed down from the seat, the engine noise providing cover for our conversation.

"Any news on Griffin?" was the first thing that he asked me.

"He was in surgery the last I heard."

He nodded and sighed deeply then moved his eyes over the rubble of the barn. "I cut him down before they got here, Ty. Before the roof fell in."

"Alive?"

"He was when the medics carted him away."

"Better than he deserved."

He pulled a red bandana from the back pocket of his jeans, wiped the perspiration from his forehead, and spread a greasy trail of ash across the mark it had imprinted on his brow. He jerked his chin in the direction of my house.

"They gonna want to talk to us?"

"Yes," I said. "After they finish speaking with the girls."

"What do you want us to say?"

I smiled and clapped him on the shoulder, and felt more tired than I had in a long, long time.

"Just tell them what happened, Caleb."

He seemed to consider that for a minute, stuffed the bandana into his pocket, and climbed back up into the tractor's seat.

"I don't suppose I need to mention the thing with the breed bull," he said.

"You can probably skip past some of the details if you want to."

———

IT WAS nearly noon by the time they finished taking statements from Jesse and my daughter. I sat beside them the entire time, hearing for the first time the personal accounts of their ordeal. Jesse's voice was leavened with emotion and my heart broke just a little while she recounted the whole story, twisting her wedding ring on her finger, her eyes glued to the floor. It broke a little more when I listened to my little girl. Cricket's jaw was set like stone, her posture as erect as if she had been balancing a bowl of boiling water on her head. She never even glanced at her mother or at me the entire time she spoke, her fingers interlaced into a ball, and I wondered if the images that lived inside her head would ever leave her. I recognized the self-indulgence of that thought the very instant that it crossed my mind and I felt a sense of shame wash over me that ached just like a bone bruise.

The investigator thanked them as they packed their gear and left. None of us stood up or said a word. Wyatt shuffled in as the front door closed behind them, his midsection shaved and taped and bandaged where he'd absorbed the vicious strikes from his family's attackers. He curled up at my feet and closed his eyes.

I don't know how long we sat there, but when I came back to myself, I found that Cricket had been staring at my face.

"Let's take a drive," I said to her. "Let's go do something good."

Her eyes softened just a little, and she smiled.

———

THE SKY was ribbed with diaphanous clouds that looked like spilled cream, or the silt and salt marks left behind on sand from a receding tide. I tuned the truck's radio to the only station I could find that played music, and turned it down low to fill in the silence. Cricket's gaze was transfixed by something far in the distance, and she was idly twisting a lock of her hair on her finger as she frequently had done as a child. I thought she said something, but I didn't quite catch it, so I reached over and switched off the radio.

"Did you say something?"

She turned in her seat and shifted her focus on me.

"I don't feel anything," she said. "It seems like I should, but I don't."

I knew exactly what she meant, but some thoughts need to be aired out in daylight, or they'll start to fester and rot inside your head.

"I killed somebody. But I don't have any feelings about it."

I could have elected to be charitable and tell her that some people were simply different from out of the womb, but that's not the belief that I held to; my experience taught me that most men embraced whatever evils they practiced out of choice.

"You didn't kill anybody," I said. "Those men were born dead."

She chewed at a rough edge on her thumbnail and her eyes slid sideways, out through the windshield.

"Shouldn't there be something?"

"You think there should be because you are good, Cricket. But what you did last night was a public service. They would have hurt you and your mother; don't hold on to any reservations about that."

She crossed her legs, Indian style, on the bench seat and pressed her back against the door.

"You don't need to convince me, I was there."

"If I had been there, I would have done the same thing and never thought twice," I said. "You need to make me a promise. If you ever do start to feel anything remotely like guilt or remorse, you call me so I can remind you that you're wrong."

Her lips turned up at the corners and she wiped at a dewdrop of moisture that had pooled up at the edge of her eye.

"You'd like that, wouldn't you," she said. "To remind me I'm wrong."

I reached across the width of the seat and squeezed her hand.

"Only about that."

———

A FEW minutes later I turned off the road and drove the narrow dirt track that opened onto the place that belonged to Teresa Pineu. Cricket sat up straight in her seat, cranked down the window, and leaned her head out.

"Where'd everybody go?" she said.

The fields where the protestors had once camped were abandoned and resembled a wasteland left behind after a battle. Loose garbage rolled over the broken soil like tumbleweeds, a patchwork of mud-soiled blankets and the remnants of small fires that had been ringed by circles of small stones. The donated outhouses had been carted off, but the dirt underneath where they once stood was marked by puddles of filth and blue dye from the chemical toilets.

Only two people remained at the far end of the property, squatting beside a small cookfire and stirring the contents of an enamel pot they had set on a square of chain-link fence laid across a bed of smoldering coals. Cast-off sheets of paper and patches of cloth flapped in the wind, tangled inside the thorned vines of berries that grew wild along the shoulder of a drainage ditch.

"It looks like the day after Woodstock," I said.

Cricket ducked her head back inside the window and gaped at me.

"Why are you looking at me like that?" I said. "I go to the movies."

I pulled the truck to a stop at the foot of the stairs that led up to the front door of Teresa's trailer. She stepped out onto the landing and leaned on the rail and watched us climb out.

"The first BLM trucks started packing out this morning," she said. "Where are the news crews for that part of the story? I guess this is what victory looks like."

"So it's over?" Cricket asked.

"Still working out the details."

Cricket looked at Teresa and said, "This is depressing."

Teresa's eyes followed the taillights of a departing eighteen-wheeler. "Demonstrations are apparently more interesting than the outcome."

"You did a good thing," I told her. "We'll be your witnesses."

The flag clipped to the flagpole Teresa had nailed to the wall snapped in the breeze, and she looked as though she might start to cry. What had begun with a phone call—initiated by a woman whose heart and concern was the preservation of a herd of wild horses—had been co-opted by the acts and ambitions of the daughters and sons of political patronage; semiprofessional agitators had hijacked her cause for their own meretricious objectives.

"They broke into my home while I was up in Salem," she said. "Can you believe that?"

"I'm sorry, Teresa," I said.

"At least the storm never arrived."

"Not the one with the rain," I said and cast my eyes across the churned-up soil of her fields. "Let us help you clean this place up."

—⁓—

WE WORKED all afternoon, until the last of the rubbish had been forked into one of the rusted oil barrels we used to incinerate the debris. Teresa brought a six-pack of beer from her trailer and the three of us drank while we watched the embers rise out of the flames and roil away.

"I'm sorry," she said. "It's all I can offer."

Teresa pulled Cricket toward her, and held her tight to her chest. Their eyes were wet when they finally let go, and I reached out a hand for Teresa. I kissed her on both cheeks and she waved from the top step of her porch as she watched Cricket and me climb into the truck and make the long drive back to the ranch.

"You look disappointed," I said, and turned my headlights on.

"I guess I am," Cricket said. "It's not what I expected."

Cricket's long hair feathered her face in the stream of chill air. She corralled it with one hand at the back of her head and rolled up the window with the other. The silence inside the cab was sudden.

"I'm not disappointed, I'm angry," she said finally. "I mean, what the hell was that? Why would they do that to someone like Teresa?"

"Everybody's heard of false prophets," I said. "But nobody mentions false believers. Some people feel invisible unless they're standing up next to a spotlight."

"Or flapping their mouths. It's all bullshit."

The fence posts that marked the edge of the road were weathered gray and rotted along the saw cuts, their bases choked with mustard weeds. The quiet inside was one of the heaviest I'd ever heard.

"Those are the same people who scratch their names onto tabletops and bathroom walls," I said. "They fear it's the only lasting contribution they might ever make to this earth."

"Are you saying that's who I am?"

"I'm saying that's who you are *not*. It's the reason you have that hollow feeling inside you. It's the reason you befriended the boys who were making their film. It's the reason you respect Teresa Pineu."

I hadn't yet told Cricket about the murders of Peter and Sly, and I judged this to be neither the time nor the circumstance to change that. For the moment, their memory was better served this way.

Her eyes drifted over the landscape and landed on a small herd of blacktails grazing inside a fenced orchard, then she leaned her head on the window and sighed.

"Are you all right, Cricket?"

"I will be," she said.

———◦◦◦———

THE HOUSE smelled of bleach and the rugs had been rolled up and removed. The bullet hole that had spidered the bay window had been covered over with squares of cardboard Jesse had taped to either side.

"The glazier is coming down from Lewiston tomorrow," she said when she saw me eyeing the glass.

Framed photographs and artwork rested on the floor beneath wet spots that marked where the walls had been recently scrubbed. The sleeves of my old faded snap-button shirt that she used when she worked were rolled up past her elbows. Her hair was tied back in a ponytail, loose strands framing her face.

"How is Teresa?" she asked Cricket. "She must be over the moon."

"Everyone's gone. Everybody."

"I thought it would be like the Fourth of July down there," Jesse said.

She came out of the kitchen and into the living room, drying her hands on a dishcloth.

"So did I."

"That's like leaving the game during the seventh-inning stretch."

"They vandalized her home while she was away," Cricket added.

"What's wrong with people?"

Cricket slid her hands into the pockets of her blue jeans and shook her head.

"People are really beginning to piss me off," Cricket said.

I grilled steaks and ears of early corn in the husk while my daughter and wife showered and changed. I had just taken them out of the fire when the phone rang.

"Do you recognize my voice, Mr. Dawson? If you do, please don't say it aloud."

"Yes."

"Can you meet me tomorrow morning around ten? There's something I need to show you."

"What's—"

"Meet me at that place where you found Dub Naylor," he said. "Roger that?"

"I'll be there," I said and hung up.

"Smells good," Jesse said as she tipped up on her toes and kissed me. "Who was that on the phone?"

"Rex Blackwood."

Her eyes went momentarily dark.

"What did he want?"

"He wants to meet me tomorrow, up on the North Camp pasture."

She cocked her head sideways and looked in my eyes. The smile that animated her features was not the same one that had been there before.

"Why there?"

"I don't know."

"Are you going?"

"Of course, I'm going."

"That man scares the hell out of me."

"At least he called this time."

We ate on the plank table out on the porch, by the light of a pair of brass oil lamps whose rims had gone dusky with soot, and the fragrance of wild hyacinth Jesse had picked and placed in a vase. When we had finished, I did the dishes while the girls watched TV. It almost seemed normal, except for the odd lapses of quiet and the sense we were all trying too hard.

I hadn't slept in nearly two days and my eyesight had begun to go soft at the edges, my mind pulling loose at the moorings like a tent whose stake poles had come out of the ground and left the flap snapping loose on the wind. Cricket stayed up and watched TV in the dark while Jesse and I went to our room.

I propped a Winchester in the corner, arm's reach from my side of the bed.

"Is that going to bother you?" I asked.

Jesse pulled back the covers and showed me a hard look.

"I'm not one of those women, Ty," she said. "We all did what had to be done."

"I meant no insult."

"I know you didn't," she said and the ice in her eyes melted away. "We don't need to give grief a second show in our lives by talking about it. It's over."

I slid under the covers and twisted the knob on the lamp.

Jesse crawled in close beside me and nested her head on my chest. She kissed me and said, "Go to sleep."

CHAPTER TWENTY-TWO

CRICKET WAS ALREADY awake when I came into the kitchen for coffee. She was wearing blue-and-black checked men's flannel pajamas and a pair of old sheepskin-lined moccasins, and looked like she had been up for a while.

"Couldn't sleep?" I asked and gave her a kiss on the crown of her head.

"I saw it on the news last night. Peter and Sly were murdered by the side of some road."

"I'm sorry, Cricket. I couldn't find the right time to tell you."

Her lips tightened into a line, but there was neither anger nor bitterness in her expression.

"There is no right time," she said softly.

Cricket stepped past me and poured coffee from the percolator and studied the cream that she swirled into the cup. She held it tight in the palms of both hands and blew at the steam as it rose.

"I'm sorry," I said lamely. "They were good kids."

"Yeah, they were. I'm sorry too. Seems like there's plenty to be sorry about these days."

The sky was deep blue outside the window, and I heard the birds light in the willow and the wet gargle of redwings hunting for food.

"Give me a minute to get dressed," she said. "I'll come out and help you saddle the horse."

She padded out of the kitchen and I thought I heard the sound of a car pull up into the driveway. Wyatt straggled out from his bed in the mudroom, wagged his tail, and followed me out to the porch.

A man stepped out of a familiar dark-colored Dodge Coronet and stood at the base of the stairs. He took off the Madison hat he'd been wearing and tossed it on the seat.

"I thought you'd want to know that the four suspects—the ones who survived their confrontation with you—have been transferred to the hospital ward at the state pen up in Salem."

"Good morning, Conrad," I said. "Coffee?"

"They're being held without bail while we sort out jurisdiction and charges. A couple of them have warrants out in several separate states."

"Oregon has the death penalty," I said. "Make sure they stay here to stand trial."

"We followed up on your lead, and the Idaho State Troopers located the fugitive from the Skadden killings," he said. He buttoned his suit jacket and took his eyes off me to stare at the shine on his shoes.

"They found him in a twelve-room motel about 400 miles from here, just over the border near Potlatch," he said. "The guy had shaved off his hair and his beard in an attempt to alter his appearance, but it obviously hadn't been enough."

"Enough for what?" I said and took a sip of my coffee. Wyatt rubbed up against the shank of my boots to scratch an itch under the gauze.

"He took three shots to the back of his head from a .22-caliber handgun, execution style. The pistol had been wiped down and left on the dresser at the scene."

"And the saddlebags? The money?"

"What money?"

"Are you sure you don't want some coffee?"

Averill Conrad cocked his head and looked first at the dog, then at me.

"They didn't find anything but the guy's bike and his clothes. Repeat what you said about money."

"I didn't say anything. Forget it."

Conrad stepped back and placed one hand on the door latch of his car and looked like he was about to get in. He stopped himself and looked into my face.

"I'm not a huge admirer of yours, or of this situation, Mr. Dawson."

"Remind me about that the next time I see you," I said. "I'll let you know if I give a goddamn by then. Thanks just the same for dropping by."

———

A BLANKET of late-morning ground fog lay over the floor of the valley, obscuring all but the tallest of trees, and put me in mind of a vast silver lake as I rode my horse up the trail to the North Pasture. I topped the last rise and reined to a stop in a circle of sunbreak that passed between dew-laden branches and felt its warmth spread on the back of my coat. I studied the deep purple creases etched into the mountains and the narrow striations of snow that remained at the high elevations. Somewhere inside the cedars, a scrub jay mimicked the cry of a circling hawk.

I had arrived early, and no one was there when I finally broke out of the old growth and onto the flat of the meadow. The horses that Caleb had earlier herded here from the barn were lazily grazing in new grass that had grown well past their ankles. I watered the one that I had been riding at the steel tank near the base of the eclipse windmill, then loosened the cinch and removed the saddle and blanket and bridle and leaned them against the trunk of a tree. I turned him loose to graze with the others while I spoke with Blackwood, intending to round up Drambuie and ride him back home when this meeting was concluded.

I lit up a smoke and unhooked my pistol belt from the pommel and buckled it on as I watched a cloud pass between me and the sun. As one, the herd raised their heads from the grass and turned their attention skyward, their ears cocked forward in alarm. I reached for the rifle tucked in its scabbard and scanned the edge of the meadow for coyotes or whatever had put a spook in the animals. Seconds later, I heard the dull thrum of an aircraft engine dopplering closer and the silhouette of a helicopter drifted toward me from over the tops of the trees. The wash from the rotors flattened the grass near the pond where I had found Dub Naylor's body, several hundred yards away. I pressed the butt of my cigarette into the wet soil and walked toward the descending chopper with my rifle held close against my chest.

The engine flared as the skids touched the ground and a door disengaged on the copilot's side. It was a Bell UH-1, the type that had come to be known as a Huey, but this one had been painted a deep matte gray, nearly black, and bore no identifying marks of any kind whatsoever, not even numbers on the tail. I saw a man step down from the cockpit, hunch underneath the decelerating whirl of the blades, and jog toward where I stood with my back pressed against the rough bark of a conifer.

Rex Blackwood slid off the mirrored sunglasses he wore and grinned at me from under the brim of a faded ball cap with an STP logo patch stitched to the crown. The engines idled down to a dull throb and he reached into the pocket of a military field jacket and pulled out a handful of hard candy mints wrapped in cellophane and offered one to me.

"Want one?" he asked. "I woke up this morning and my mouth tasted like I ate a skunk's ass."

"Do you ever wonder if there's something wrong with you?" I asked, and declined the candy.

"Every goddamn day."

"Want to tell me what we're doing out here?" I said. "And who that thing belongs to."

"The bird?"

"Yes, the bird."

"It belongs to the company I work for," he said. "And the truth is, I'm not really supposed to be here, but there's a few things I think you deserve to know."

"The *company* you work for?"

"Small 'c.' I'm not with the Agency."

I searched his face with renewed interest; Blackwood had slid into and out of my field of focus over the past several days, his behavior and dress like that of some kind of chameleon. Though I had no reason to trust what he'd just told me, his eyes held no trace of the moral vacuity I had come to associate with Company men.

"Here's the deal, Dawson," he said, gauging the doubt he had seen in my expression. "I work for a private organization that investigates anomalies."

"Anomalies," I repeated.

"Weird shit that crops up out of the blue. Some call them 'Black Swan Events.'"

"I know what an anomaly is."

His eyes squinted past me and he watched the horses graze in the meadow. "Thing is, you've been smack in the center of one. You were set up to fail, but you didn't."

"I am aware of that now," I said. "Who set me up?"

"You already know the answer."

"Say the name."

"The late Sheriff Lloyd Skadden."

"And what do you know about a fugitive biker with a face that looks like a pockmarked rabbit? He acquired three holes in the back of his head in a shitbag motel room in Idaho."

"I heard about that."

"And the cash he was carrying?"

"I don't involve myself in that sort of work," Blackwood said, taking his eyes off the horses and turning them back on me. "Let's take a ride."

I had heard stories of Vietcong prisoners of war being interrogated at high altitudes and shoved out the cargo doors of choppers that looked much like the one that was now parked in my pasture.

"I can see the wheels turning in your head, Mr. Dawson. I don't participate in the kinds of things you're considering right now. Not anymore."

"Odin gave an eye for the acquisition of knowledge."

Blackwood smiled again, rocked back on his heels, and looked down at the toes of his boots.

"I like that you have an appreciation of mythology," he said. "But I'm not asking the payment of any kind of toll. Bring your sidearm with you if it makes you feel any better. And you can sit in the backseat so there's nobody behind you."

He started to walk toward the chopper, but I remained planted where I stood. After a few steps he looked at me over his shoulder.

"I don't have much time, Dawson," he said. "Like I told you before, I'm not supposed to be here at all."

———⁕———

BLACKWOOD STRAPPED himself into the copilot's seat, and I took the one directly behind the pilot, diagonal to Blackwood so I could keep an eye on him. Like its exterior, the interior of the chopper had been modified for paramilitary use, and had been outfitted with two rows of plush leather passenger seats.

The cargo bay, however, was arrayed with electronic equipment and drop-down net seating and gear hooks that could easily accommodate a tactical team and mission matériel.

"Put those cans on your ears," Blackwood said as he slipped a pair of headphones over the crown of his ball cap. He pulled down a small L-shaped arm from one of the earpieces and positioned a small microphone in front of his lips.

"Speak into the mic there on the side," he added. "It can get pretty noisy in here."

The pilot spun up the rotors and we rose from the ground and peeled off at a sickening angle. I looked down through the plexiglass window and watched as we passed over the fence line that had so recently been ploughed over and repaired at least twice that I knew of. A few minutes later I recognized the blackened circle of ash where I had stumbled upon the remains of one my strays when riding out here with Peter and Sly.

The pilot swung a wide half-circle over the sheer canyon walls and dipped down low over the alluvial rock fan that I had previously only seen from ground level. He slowed as we turned toward the narrow mouth of the crevasse and hovered momentarily before we moved into the shadows.

"Do you know this place?" Blackwood asked. His voice sounded tinny and distant inside my headphones.

"I've only been here once before."

"What did you see?"

"I can't really say for sure," I said. "It looked like a building. A fairly large metal building."

Blackwood nodded and gestured up into the gorge. The pilot swung sideways so I could get a better view out my window.

"What do you see now?"

I placed a hand across my brow as a shield from the glare and squinted into the deep shade.

"Nothing," I said. "Nothing at all."

"Take a look down below us," Blackwood said.

"I don't see anything."

"Not even one scrap of rubbish or animal sign. No tire tracks. No sign of habitation at all. For a place where you claim a building once stood, that's kind of strange, wouldn't you say?"

The pilot gained altitude and swung southward, in the direction of my house and my ranch. He moved swiftly and high enough so the noise of the engine would be minimized at ground level. The pilot traced a circle over the Corcoran place and we followed the fence that marked off the border between the BLM land and the Diamond D. We flew more slowly as we headed in a generally northern direction and Blackwood swiveled to face me again.

"I want you to look down and make a mental note as to where you found the remains of your cattle," he said. "Tell me if you notice a pattern."

About ten minutes later, we returned to the North Camp where the pilot set the chopper down in the grass. Blackwood made a circling gesture with his index finger, removed his headphones, opened his door, and got out. I did the same on my side, ducked low under the rotors, and we both jogged back to the tree line.

"Every one of the carcasses was within twenty or so feet of my fence."

Blackwood nodded.

"I would suspect that if you marked their positions on a map," he said. "You'd find that they run in a line, straight up the same longitude."

I wasn't grasping his point, but the message was clear. This was obviously neither a rustling nor a random occurrence.

"I don't take your meaning," I admitted.

"I need to tell you a story," he said.

CHAPTER TWENTY-THREE

"WHO'S GOING TO answer for the death of Dub Naylor?" I asked after Blackwood had finished.

"Nobody. You'll never identify the one who did it."

"That's unacceptable."

"That's the way that it is," Blackwood said. "Think of Dub Naylor as the first casualty in a war that won't be declared and will never be given a name."

According to Blackwood, the building I had seen buried deep in the shadows of that narrow box canyon was a temporary facility built by a private military contractor for the purpose of testing what he called Unmanned Aerial Vehicles. Dub Naylor had apparently passed through the rotted section of fence that the cattle had pushed over, in his attempt to round up my strays. In the process, he had followed the cows all the way to the cliff's edge, much like I had done with Peter and Sly, but had been killed by sharpshooters tasked with the responsibility of securing the facility's secret. Fearing that if one of my men simply went missing, it would draw far more prolonged law enforcement attention than one who had been murdered in a manner they knew would go unsolved. They relocated his body back to my ranch, where Dub would eventually be found, and the investigation would proceed under the supervision of Lloyd Skadden; the contractor had long had the sheriff in its employ.

"I knew a guy in the navy," Blackwood said. "He died of ptomaine poisoning while on leave in Saipan. The thing about that kind of death is that the incubation period is so long that you never associate the actual cause of the illness with the item consumed. You understand what I'm telling you?"

The original intent of the development of the UAVs had sprung from a practical need: the collection of reconnaissance photos for use by intelligence and military agencies. They could fly at high altitude with an insignificant noise profile, and do so without placing the lives of actual pilots at risk. Then the corporation got creative. If the craft could collect photographs, why could it not be adapted to deploy munitions with equal success? The limits of its potential for use on the battlefield, not to mention pinpointed political assassinations, were unimaginable. Of course, if word of the technology leaked, the strategic advantage would be lost. The development of this weapon, as with any secret weapon, had to remain strictly covert. It couldn't be tested out in the open, so even remote military installations were out of the question for that purpose. This had been created by the private sector, after all. As a result, once the vehicle was ready for real-world experimentation they constructed a temporary facility in the middle of the last place anybody would think to look. Meriwether County was perfect. There was only one road in and out of the valley and the livestock population outnumbered humans fifty-to-one.

"The canyon is narrow, and runs north to south," Blackwood said. "Given the trajectory of the sun, the entire structure would lay hidden in shadow for all but fifteen minutes a day, with ample space for a runway that was essentially an extinct river fan."

"They shot my cows with the thing?"

"At some point, they had to test its efficiency on something that was actually alive."

"Why bring me into it at all? I'm just a rancher."

His eyes fell on the pack of cigarettes tucked into my shirt pocket.

"Mind if I bum one of those things?" Blackwood asked.

I shook one out of the pack for him and passed him my lighter. He crouched down on his haunches and angled his back to the wind. I lit one myself and waited while he gathered his thoughts.

"Who better than you?" he said as he exhaled. "From the contractor's point of view, it was a twofer: You'd be distracted from pursuing your cattle-killing problem, while at the same time creating the illusion that law enforcement was on top of the growing unrest at Teresa Pineu's."

My eyes wandered over the newly repaired stretch of barbed-wire fence and wondered how much of this might have been avoided but for a handful of dry-rotted posts.

"The contractor was facing a serious problem," Blackwood continued. "They had to bug out, and get it done quickly and quietly. Your cattle mysteriously exploding had not been good for business. When your friend the wild-horse advocate started raising a ruckus at the opposite end of the valley they saw their opportunity and took it."

"A head fake."

"If they could keep the eyes and ears of the public trained on the south end of the county, they could exfiltrate out of the north end without attracting any notice. They didn't need more than a few days to pack up and disappear, and they had the sheriff bought and paid for to orchestrate a distraction."

"Skadden called in the Charlatans himself."

Blackwood nodded and picked a loose piece of tobacco off his tongue.

"He had to be sure things came completely undone. It was working fairly well until the bikers started working off-script."

"Christ," I said. "Emily Meeghan."

Blackwood nodded again.

"And Peter and Sly."

"The two kids shooting the movie," Blackwood said. "That hit was intentional. Those boys had the facility on the footage they shot when they went riding out here with you."

A wave of nausea passed through me. I had been the one who placed the call and informed Skadden that they had been up here shooting film.

He read my expression and said, "Don't blame yourself. Skadden already knew about it."

"If you knew this shit, why didn't you stop it?"

He tilted his head sideways and looked directly into my eyes.

"I didn't arrive here with the knowledge I am sharing with you now. I put it all together, same as you."

"Not all of it."

"Fair enough," he said. "But to be clear, the only information I had that you didn't was the existence of the test facility—that and the fact that some rancher's cows were exploding for no reason. It's why they sent me out here in the first place."

"You could have said something."

"It's not my mandate. The organization I work for has a strict noninterventionist policy. Are you familiar with the Observer Effect?" Blackwood pushed his hands deep into the pockets of his field jacket and gazed into the valley. "There are physicists where I work who are convinced that even someone's *thoughts* can alter the outcome of an event. The men I work for concern themselves far more with 'what' and 'who' rather than 'why.' It's the way they make their money."

"Your terminology can be a little vexing," I said. "Blood doesn't just rinse off."

My tone was bitter, but Blackwood ignored it.

"You and your family are good people, and I don't like seeing good people placed in the crosshairs for no reason. We're going to stop talking about me now."

My stomach churned and the back of my throat felt like I had swallowed battery acid.

"Why tell me any of this?"

"'In for a penny in for a pound' and all that," he said while he stubbed and fieldstripped his cigarette butt. "As we've both come to understand, you were set up to fail from the beginning, Mr. Dawson. The demonstrations at the Pineu place were supposed to devolve into a full-scale goatfuck just like Wounded Knee or Kent State and they could lay the blame on you. But the bikers went off the reservation, and if you hadn't stopped them and calmed the protest, the south end of your valley would have gone up in flames. That is not hyperbole. I had your back as best as I could."

"Within limits."

He studied my face for a long moment before he replied.

"Limits that I exceeded," he said finally. "You couldn't be everywhere at once, Mr. Dawson, so I helped you the only way I could."

"What happens now?"

"I disappear."

"And all of the other bullshit? The unmanned spy planes?"

"UAVs."

"Whatever."

"The genie is out of the bottle," he said. "The idiots in DC believe they have the power and the means to alter the nature of war, that in the future it can be waged via remote control. They believe in some imaginary misguided honor inherent in rules of engagement against enemy combatants who don't recognize rules. They believe they can send our soldiers to fight

wars inside countries without collateral damage or pissing off
the local establishment. They believe they can engage in polite
little wars."

"I can't accept that explanation," I said.

"You'd better accept *this*: Every last politician in Washing-
ton has nothing but pig shit inside his skull. These flying toys
here? They'll end up using them for things you truly do not
want to contemplate. Sure, at first they'll deploy them to kill
a few bad guys, but eventually they'll also use them to do shit
like trying to control the weather, or surveil you while you
live your daily life, or keep track of the purchases you make
at the liquor store or pharmacy. They will tell you that their
mission and motivation is to keep the public safe, but that is
a lie and could not be further from the truth. This is only the
beginning. You and I won't even recognize this world thirty
years from now."

He stood up and offered his hand to me. I shook it and
saw something else form up behind his eyes, but he caught
himself short and moved to turn away.

"Say it, Blackwood," I said.

He dipped into his pocket, unwrapped the cellophane
from another mint candy, and popped it into his mouth.

"Do you believe a man must sometimes do bad things in
order to do good?" he asked. "That is not a rhetorical question."

"I don't know how to answer that."

He smiled, took off his ball cap, and slapped the dust off
the knees of his pants with the crown.

"Good luck," I said.

"You too," he said and walked slowly back to the chopper.
He made the circling gesture with his finger again, and the
pilot spun up the rotors.

"Take care of yourself, Mr. Dawson."

—∽∾∿∾∽—

I WALKED out into the meadow and whistled for Drambuie, watched as he raised his head and pricked his ears forward and ambled through the tall grass toward me. I stroked his neck and spoke softly while he stood patiently waiting for the saddle.

The silence closed in on me in the wake of Blackwood's departure, and an entirely new set of depressing thoughts crowded my head. The massive tectonic shifts that created this valley took place over a period of tens of thousands of years, a shifting of subsurface plates initiated by earthquakes and volcanic eruptions that raised mountains and redirected the courses of rivers, globe-altering events that can be expressed only in terms of geological time. But modern man, in the profligate expression of his vanity, had come to expect that the fruits of his fantasies must be realized inside the course of his own lifetime.

Those in positions of power and authority used to concern themselves with violations of the public trust. But once that trust no longer exists, what is left to violate?

In an expression of my own petty vanity, I believed I had chosen a path for my life that might somehow be less malevolent in its nature. The methods and manner of ranching had remained largely unchanged for the last hundred years, as did the appeal of its agrarian nature for me. Apart from the advent of railroads and eighteen-wheeled trucks supplanting months-long cattle drives, this business was as it had been in my grandfather's time, and change for its own sake was viewed to be as pointless and fickle as fashion. I had held fast onto notions of character and honor that I once thought to be timeless, and believed I could be the final holdout if need be.

I was mistaken.

NEW YEAR'S
1974

SAMUEL GRIFFIN SPENT several weeks of recovery in the guest room at our house. Jesse or I would drive him daily up to Lewiston for physical therapy, and I never once heard him complain. At his insistence, he moved down to the bunkhouse when he no longer used a cane, and though he still walked with a slight limp, his physician assured us all that it would pass with time.

I was asked to stay on as acting sheriff of Meriwether County until a proper election could be arranged. Jordan Powell and Sam Griffin volunteered to remain with me as deputies, even though both would have preferred to be setting a horse or even bucking hay.

Jesse and I were enjoying a night out on the town at the newly remodeled Cotton Blossom bar when I learned from Lankard Downing that I had won the election as an unwarned and unsuspecting write-in candidate. For the third time that year I'd been conscripted to serve in a position I had neither sought nor wanted, and Lankard stood a round of drinks for the house in my honor. As I mentioned before, he loved nothing more than to disseminate unpleasant news.

—◈◈◈—

ONE DAY in late summer, Jesse and I rode our horses all the way out to a disused line camp called *Amantes* at the westernmost edge of the ranch. Because of its distance from headquarters, a water well had been sunk and a small cabin constructed to accommodate the cowhands during Spring Works and autumn roundups. By late morning we had ridden several miles down through the creases of low hills and cut creeks and the air smelled of dust and sun-heated rocks, and the chaff from the cottonwoods fell down and swirled on the wind.

I swung out of the saddle and handed the reins to Jesse while I unhooked a wire and held open the gate. Jesse and her horse moved into the pasture, trailing Drambuie behind.

We ate a picnic lunch in the shade beside a pond strung with cattails and long grass. Dragonflies circled and dipped on the still surface where a large boulder had rolled down and lodged in the mud. We spoke about Cricket, and the interest she had taken in her job that summer, working for Jesse as a location scout for a Hollywood western being shot on a studio back lot somewhere in Southern California. A new sense of determination and gravity had replaced the pious and whimsical idealism that had defined her just a few months earlier, a remnant of spring '73 that would always remain a part of her makeup, like a broken frame that had been put back together and replaced on the wall.

A couple hours later Jesse and I passed through a clearing and came to the thick copse of trees beyond which stood the lodgepole archway and hinge gate that marked the entrance to *Amantes* camp. The shadows had grown long in the afternoon sun and my attention had drifted to the sky overhead and the cries of a red-tailed hawk being mobbed by a trio of grackles.

I was nearly thrown from my saddle when Drambuie spooked sideways, pitched his head wildly, and lifted his head to the wind. His ears angled forward, his nostrils flared as I regained control and saw that Jesse's horse had begun to crow-hop and she turned him away from the fence.

We walked the horses back toward the trees, where we gave them time to calm themselves. Jesse climbed down and led her mount a short distance away. I dismounted too and asked Jesse to keep hold of the horses while I went on foot to investigate the source of their unease.

The tall stalks of brown grass grew to my waist, and bent over on their stems in currents pushed by the hot breeze. It was not until I had nearly reached the swing gate that I saw a form stretched out prostrate on the ground. Even before I stooped to check the old man's pulse, I knew that Eli Corcoran was dead.

He was lying facedown, and I knelt in the dirt beside him, wavered a moment before I rolled him over. The blue of his eyes had faded and his skin had gone waxen and cool to the touch. The wind pulled at the loose collar of his shirt and I studied the peaceful expression on his unshaven face and wondered where his spirit might have gone. There was no sign of the haunted look he had worn when I had last seen him, and I prayed he was no longer a lonely old man, but instead a young maverick pushing a herd up to Abilene or torturing the truth beside a fire ringed with stones, and passing a bottle of mescal from hand to hand somewhere out along the Chisholm.

The rusted chain that held the gate shut dangled in the dirt where he'd dropped it, and I spotted his horse in the distance, outlined against the bright sky, wandering aimlessly and dragging his reins through the weeds at the crest of the hill. I was sure Eli had set off from his place on some grand adventure, preparing to raise hell and high cotton with the wild-eyed boys of his youth that only still existed in his mind. He hadn't died on my ranch, he had died with his friends somewhere out under the stars.

Jesse came up behind me. She had left our horses tied to a tree limb downwind and well off in the distance. She knelt by my side, placed her open palm across the stillness of his heart and exhaled a ragged sigh. My eyes burned wetly when I lifted my head to look at her.

"What happened to him, Ty?" she asked, and the wind blew a stray lock of hair across her cheek.

"No violence came to him," I said. "He just lived himself out."

———

TERESA PINEU'S notoriety faded just as rapidly as it had bloomed, which was fine as far as she was concerned, if you took the time to ask her. She resumed her work as a horse trainer, forgotten by the horde that had descended on her ranch only to disappear to some other destination to chant the slogans of some other cause.

The events that followed in the wake of the Wounded Knee occupation, however, were far more tragic. On May 8, after a siege that lasted seventy-one days, the militants surrendered to the feds. During that time, 500,000 rounds of ammunition had been expended by both sides in exchanges of gunfire that claimed the lives of two Sioux men and wounded several federal agents. Eleven townspeople had been taken hostage, and 600 occupiers arrested. Of that 600, none was ever convicted of a crime, and the movement's leader, Russell Means, was acquitted of all charges and set free after a federal judge determined that the government had unlawfully mishandled both evidence and witnesses.

After all was said and done, the Pine Ridge Indian Reservation suffered a legacy of violence that continued on for years. The community remained among the poorest in the nation, and the murder rate was nearly three times greater than that in Detroit, Michigan. Not one of the occupiers' demands was ever meaningfully met.

—⁓⁓⁓—

BY MID-OCTOBER, the trees had lost their leaves and Cricket had returned to school. I spent eleven days in a Salem courtroom, including two full days of testimony, at the conclusion of which three of the four bikers who had been awaiting trial in the state penitentiary received twenty-five-year sentences for arson, rape, unlawful sexual penetration, aggravated battery, and assault. Due to the incompetence of both the DA and the medical examiner, they could not bring a murder charge against any of them, despite the cruel and savage circumstances in the deaths of Peter Davis and Sylvester "Sly" McCarty. The fourth Charlatan, the racist waste of skin I referred to as Wallace, was extradited to Nevada where he will likely face the gas chamber after standing trial on three separate counts of murder, the details of which are each too pointless and gruesome to describe.

As Rex Blackwood had predicted, no one ever was indicted for the killing of Dub Naylor, the responsibility for which I lay squarely at the feet of Denton Lowell, the spineless district attorney for Meriwether County, and the medical examiner, Dr. Gerald Hill.

The ME kept his job, as there aren't yet any laws on the books with respect to being a toady, turd, and dumbshit; but Denton Lowell resigned at the conclusion of the trial beneath a well-founded dark cloud of suspicion. He had been a close personal friend of Sheriff Lloyd Skadden's, which at a minimum suggests he possessed the moral clarity and the intellect of an earthworm.

Emily Meeghan spent nearly three months in a psychiatric clinic outside of Portland. She spends her time these days working at her father's feedstore, and every now and then she will show me a vague smile of recognition when she sees me at their store, or at the counter drinking coffee at Rowan Boyle's diner. I've had to lock up her dad once or twice for drunk and disorderly behavior, but we've kept it local, and I think he's getting a handle on it now. The whole town of Meridian, myself included, tends to give him wide latitude on his outbursts, which have never featured violence directed at anyone other than himself.

I continued working with the ODOJ and together we won an indictment against Oregon State Trooper Wilkens and two others who were also in the pocket of the military contractor which had been funneling protection money through Lloyd Skadden. All three were sent to prison. I have not yet been able to identify the firm by name, but the case will remain open on my desk until the damage they have caused in the lives of Dub Naylor and his family and so many others in my county has been rectified.

In short, the elected officials we had previously entrusted with their positions had proven themselves unworthy not only of the public's confidence, but had learned they couldn't trust themselves or one another either. They had reminded ordinary citizens that solipsism was a prerequisite, or at the very least a consequence, of bureaucratic power. There is an Oriental proverb that states, *The fall is not far for the one who flies low*. While that sentiment may contain a certain truth, I have chosen to engage my obligations at a slightly higher level, and damn the consequences.

⸻

GALILEO SAID that all truths are easy to understand once they are discerned; the point is to discern them. It has also been said that most conspiracies are conceived in hell, and rarely have angels as witnesses. I have come to learn that both statements are true.

I will always recall 1973 as the year that everything I thought I knew had changed. I suspect many others in our country may well do the same. Some believe that our nation lost its innocence on a November day in Dallas back in 1963; if it is possible to lose such a thing twice, it happened a second time, nearly eleven years later, on August 9, with the resignation of a sitting president who faced impeachment for betraying the trust of the citizens he had sworn an oath to defend and to protect.

I find myself unable to shake the imagery that the man named Blackwood had implanted in my brain: a world resembling Ouroboros bent on devouring itself alive. The rotation of the earth seemed to begin to spin more rapidly that year, and if we did not act with both immediacy and resolve we would discover far too late that we had given our lives over to a cabal of self-deifying oligarchs who had appointed themselves as saviors.

⎯⎯✺⎯⎯

CRICKET BROUGHT a friend home for the holidays, and they spent most of it riding horses, baking bread, or sitting with us in the living room next to the Christmas tree beside the fire. The season had been uncharacteristically dry, but very cold. Two days after Christmas, there was an ice storm in the night that cocooned the shrubs and tree limbs in a thin coating of frost that glowed like crystal in the sunshine and the cloudless light of the next morning.

We drank pink champagne from narrow flutes and watched the ball drop on TV on New Year's Eve. Though none of us had the temerity to say the words aloud, every one of us was more than happy to see the Old Year reach its end.

After Cricket and her friend turned in for the night, Jesse sat beside me outside on the porch swing. We wrapped ourselves beneath a heavy blanket, snug in our winter coats. The air smelled dry and sweet with fallen needles and the woodsmoke from the fire, and she leaned her head against my shoulder as we drank the last of the champagne.

"Look," Jesse said and tossed the blanket from her knees. She gripped the railing and leaned out beneath the eve, her eyes cast to the sky. I joined her there and watched the first snowflakes we'd seen all winter falling softly from the clouds.

NEW YEAR'S morning I placed a saddle on Drambuie and took a long ride alone out to the Three Roses. A thin blanket of snow still covered the ground and clung to the bare branches of deciduous trees, and the sun looked like damp golden cotton in the frigid morning air. Gray puffs of Drambuie's and my crystallized breath chained the trail at my back, and the sounds of his hooves perforating the crust on the snowfall sounded like whispers.

I turned up the narrow path that ran through that part of the glade that almost always was concealed from the sun. I felt the temperature drop as we entered the swale that had been cut through the forest by the flow of the creek and tightened the collar of my fleece-lined coat. The water was clear, transparent as glass, as it flowed over a riffle where aspens and willow trees grew close to the bank and a skin of ice had formed along its edges. In spite of the cold, I could smell lichen and cedar and the water that rolled over the pebbled streambed. A lone turtle idled on a flat rock in a fragile taper of sunlight, and somewhere deep in the old growth a wood-pecker tapped on a tree. I spoke to Drambuie as we followed the watercourse, and he cocked his ears rearward while I softly gave voice to my confessions.

That horse had always been a good listener.

ACKNOWLEDGMENTS

I OWE A sincere debt of gratitude to two fine gentlemen who provided me with some invaluable insight and background for this book: The first is Col. Ron Battersby (USAF, ret.) and Mr. Patrick Partridge, whose decades-long experience in law enforcement is simply too extensive to enumerate. Thank you both for your expertise, and your generosity with your valuable time.

Once again, to my dad, Ron Birtcher, who taught me about horses and fishing, family and life, and gave me an early appreciation for travel and the inestimable value of reading—and writing.

To Christina for her endless supply of patience and support as all these characters wander around inside my head (and our house) while the story finds its way to the page. *Aloha pau ole.*

And to my two beautiful and talented daughters, Allegra and Britton, who provide me with so much enthusiasm, encouragement, and confidence, and always manage to demonstrate the meaning of unconditional love.

Thank you, yet again, to a pair of true professionals (whom I have the distinct privilege of calling my friends), my publishers,

Martin and Judith Shepard at The Permanent Press. And that goes for you, as well, Chris Knopf.

I also get to reap the benefits of working with an incredibly patient and talented copy editor, Barbara Anderson, who once again made it all look good. And to cover artist and designer, Lon Kirschner—thanks, amigo! You two are the best.

Until next time . . .